5IVE

Published by Janine Ellis-Fynn at Smashwords

Prologue

It was cold and dark. Diane's six-year old body shivered under her thin nightdress. She prayed her mummy would come and find her soon. Before the monster came back. He had touched her in a way that made her feel confused and scared. But when she asked him to stop, he had said he would kill her.

Her foster brother, Twig had tried to stop the bad man, but he was only twelve years old so what hope did he have? Instead Simon had forced her to watch as he did horrible things to Twig.

When her mummy had told her that she had a new boyfriend she was glad that at least she would not be lonely anymore. At first, they had fun together playing hide and seek in the garden. Mummy told her that he would be her new daddy. Diane had always dreamed about having her very own daddy just like her friends at school. It made her feel sad when the daddies came to fetch their children and they would leap into their arms and chuckle with delight. She had always wondered what it would feel like to have her own daddy pick her up and swing her around the room or make blue berry pancakes with her. Diane had never known her real father as he had left when she was just a baby.

When Diane was four years old Twig had entered her life. He was an orphan and all alone in the world, so he had come to live with them. Instantly they became best friends and would spend endless hours playing games together. She liked to think of him as her real brother. They may not have shared blood, but their bond was tight. On her fifth birthday he had given her a pretty butterfly brooch which was a kaleidoscope of colour. She had worn it proudly at her party and had not taken it off for weeks. Twig and Diane had promised to be brother and sister forever and had solemnly sworn to always be there for each other no matter what. They had crossed their little pinkie fingers and promised that they would always love each other to the moon and back.

When Simon came into their lives it seemed that Twig liked him too. He would give him piggy-back rides and tickle him until he squealed like a little pig.

The abuse had started long before Diane could even understand what he was doing to her. All she knew what that he was hurting her in her private parts where mummy had said no-one should touch her. Then one night, Simon had crept into her room and held his large hand over her mouth so she could not scream. Then his hot breath had caressed her ear as he whispered 'I'm doing this because I love you. Now, be a good baby girl and help me feel better' Numb with terror, Diane had simply nodded her head as shocked tears slipped down her cheeks.

Winter turned into spring and the daffodils began to bloom in the little garden in the front of Diane's home. She liked to pick them for her mummy and put them in a vase next to her bed. Whenever she looked at the flowers the abuse was pushed into the back of her mind. When she was looking at the flowers the bad man could not hurt her.

But then Twig started to act strangely, and she knew something was very wrong with him. He was struggling with his grades at school and was being bullied. Diane had noticed that he had become very quiet and did not want to play cops and robbers so much anymore. Today she had witnessed Simon touching Twig. He had tried to fight back but Simon had tied his hands and feet together with some rope he had found in the garage.

He had then put a foul-smelling piece of cloth against her mouth and she had passed out. Now she had woken up cold and alone on the floor and it was so dark that she could not make out where she was. She figured that maybe she was locked in the basement. But where was Twig? Diane was afraid that something awful had happened to him…

The cold metal of the butcher's knife gripped in her hand felt strangely soothing against the rush of warm, sticky blood oozing from the wound on her forehead. Charlotte vowed that the next time her husband hit her; she would retaliate. As she crouched under the kitchen table, she prayed for the courage to carry out the sinister deed she had dreamed of enacting for years. She realised that it was a case of kill or be killed.

Charlotte had tried to leave Patrick on many occasions but each time he had found her and lulled her back into a false sense of security with his honey sweet words and acts of devotion. He was a charismatic and charming man on the surface. At least that is what everyone who met him thought. Through many months of psychotherapy, Charlotte had learned that her husband was a narcissist who toyed with her emotions and kept her on a relentless merry-go-round of cat and mouse.

The sound of his key turning in the lock pulled her from her thoughts. Her heart hammered in her chest as a fist of dread squeezed the breath out of her lungs. His footsteps grew louder as he walked towards the kitchen. After polishing off a bottle of whiskey, he had nipped out to the store to stock up on his rations. The fresh round of drinking would herald in another beating. But this time, she would be ready.

'Where are you, Charlotte? I haven't had my dinner yet and I'm starving.'

Patrick dumped his car keys on the kitchen table and poured himself a drink. Charlotte shifted under the table. Fear of what was to come began to snake around her, slowly suffocating her. She needed to get a grip and focus. If she allowed him to hit her again, he could kill her. The severity of the beatings was increasing. Two weeks ago, she had landed in hospital with two cracked ribs and a broken nose. There was no way she could endure it any longer. When a blow to her stomach has caused a miscarriage a year ago, something had snapped inside her. Her psyche had been hanging by a thread and she had been teetering on the brink of insanity for as long as she could remember. Like a dew drop on a fragile spider's web. One tiny gust of wind is all it would take to send it plummeting to the ground. But this exchange had held the force of a hurricane. That one fatal punch had shattered her dreams and splintered her mind. Cracked, like a broken egg. There was no going back now. Patrick was responsible for murdering her child and she would never forgive him. On that day, blind fury and hatred had been ignited within her. Soon, it grew into a consuming fire which raged day and night.

Her eyes glistened with tears as a cold shiver raced down her spine. What was she thinking? He was far too strong for her and it was likely he would overpower her. She shuddered to think about what he might do should the butcher's knife find its way into his hands.

Hiding like an errant cockroach in the shadows was not exactly a brilliant plan. But at least down here she felt a sense of safety and it allowed her time to think. The brightly coloured tablecloth hung low enough to conceal her. If she could just remain quiet for a little while, she would have the advantage over him.

'Charlotte, where are you?' Patrick's words were laced with thinly masked irritation. There was a certain tone he used when his anger was about to spew. Any minute now his volcanic temper would erupt destroying everything in its path.

Charlotte sucked a ragged breath through her teeth. Her heart pounded against her ribcage. Acidic nausea rose in her throat as she considered her options. She could wait for him to turn and walk out of the kitchen and then plunge the knife into his back. But what if he turned around?

Years before she had met Patrick, she considered herself to be a strong, courageous woman. Nothing had frightened her back then. She had a flourishing career and a healthy self-esteem. But after ten years of marriage to her abusive husband, her pride and respect hung like a tattered garment from her thin frame. She was an empty shell with no real essence. Sometimes she contemplated suicide but quickly dismissed the thought. If she killed herself, it would be ceding defeat. She may not have much dignity left but there was a shred of fight left in her.

The insistent ticking of the wall clock grated on her already frayed nerves. She could hear him gulping down his nectar of choice like a dying man feasting on his last meal. After several minutes he pulled out a chair and sat down at the kitchen table. Charlotte scuttled into the corner to escape his legs. He stretched them out and then hunched over the table. The air was thick with the smell of putrefied alcohol. Biding her time, she drew her knees to her chest and slowed her breathing. Soon he would fall into a drunken sleep and then she would know what to do next.

***

'Craig, I just have to dash down to the shops.' Jessica said jingling her car keys in her hand. 'Promise me that you will watch the girls. I won't be long.'

'Yes, of course.' He answered with a distracted air. Craig leaned back into his chair and reached for the remote control. He had been looking forward to watching the rugby all day and at last he had a quiet moment where he could indulge himself.

'Daddy, please can I go for a swim?' The couple's four-year old daughter, Amy tugged on her father's shirt, impatient to gain his attention.

'Yes, sweetie...but where is your sister? She must watch you.'

'Bethany is in her room, Daddy. I will go and call her for you.' Amy answered in her sing song little girl voice. She stomped up the stairs calling her sister's name. Craig heard the door slam as his teenage daughter reluctantly left her bedroom lair.

'Dad,' she whined. 'I was listening to my music and all I need is to babysit my little sister. She is so annoying. Why can't you do it?' Bethany stood with her hand on her hip like a school matron chastising a child.

'Don't you dare talk to me like that, young lady? It will just be for a few minutes until your mother comes home. I want to watch the rugby. Now go and put her water wings on. I am not asking you again.'

'OK, whatever!' She replied with a huff. Bethany turned on her heel dragging her little sister by the arm. 'Come on, squirt. I will take you for a swim.'

She blew impatiently into the water wings until she felt they were satisfactorily inflated. Then she pulled her sister's tiny little twig arms through the holes. 'Just paddle around on the steps, OK.'

'I will.' Amy replied with a cheeky grin. 'I am just so hot; I can't wait to get into the water.'

'You are a real little water baby, aren't you?' Bethany said. Amy ran towards the pool and then jumped onto the first step with a splash.

Desperate for her older sister's approval, she called out to her. 'I wish I were a dolphin, Beth. Then I would be able to swim all day long.' She jumped up and down, her blonde curls dancing in the afternoon sun.

Bethany strode over to the nearest lounger and positioned herself on it like a lizard on a rock. She picked up her cell phone and began to text message a friend. Keeping one eye on her sister, her fingers jabbed quickly at the screen.

Amy splashed contentedly in the water. She was never more at home than when she was swimming. It was her most enjoyable pastime and she longed for the day she could get into the pool without the water wings. One of the arm bands was biting into the soft skin of her underarm. Yanking on it, she managed to inch it down until it sat more comfortably.

The latest pop song began to blare out of Bethany's cell phone. Expecting a call from her boyfriend, she checked the screen and smiled. Maybe he would ask her out on a date. There was a movie she had been itching to see for days.

'Michael, I am so glad you called!' She said breathlessly.

The edge of the step was beckoning to Amy. She just wanted to see what it would be like to swim on the second step. She was sure she could still stand there. Inching her way towards it, she tugged at her other armband. They had to sit on her arms evenly or she would feel uncomfortable. Jumping up and down in excitement, she slipped silently over the edge of the step. Extending her legs down, she was sure she would be able to stand on her tippy toes. She kicked her legs. Now she could feel the bottom of the pool. Maybe she could get to the next step. The mere thought of it thrilled her. Then she would be able to float properly with her arm bands on. She pushed her body forward until she was hovering above the third step.

Bethany was so engrossed in her conversation with her boyfriend; she had stopped watching her sister. She threw her head back and laughed. 'You are so funny, Michael. I can't wait to see you tonight.'

This time, Amy could not feel the bottom, but she kicked her legs just like her teacher had taught her to. Now she was really swimming. She called out to Bethany.

'Look at me, Beth.' Distracted, her sister looked up and nodded. Amy was floating with the aid of her armbands, a wide smile plastered across her cherubic face. Convinced the child was safe; Bethany waved and resumed her conversation.

Before she knew it, one of Amy's water wings slipped off her arm. She kicked her legs to retrieve it as it floated out of her reach. But the harder she tried the further away it drifted. Slowly, her head was beginning to slip under the water. She spluttered as it filled her mouth.

A few minutes later, Bethany finished her conversation. 'Bye, Michael. I'll see you later.' She glanced towards the pool. In an instant, her heart stopped. A single water wing was floating on the water and the pool pump was gurgling to dispel the other one. 'Amy!'

She raced over to the pool. Her sister's tiny body lay at the bottom. Hurling herself into the water, she swam like her life depended on it. She grabbed Amy's arm and pulled her to the surface. Bethany laid her body on the side and screamed for her father.

'Daddy, daddy! Help me!'

Craig raced outside and crouched down next to his daughter. Blind terror rose in his throat like a freight train through a tunnel. 'Phone 999! Quickly, Beth.' He opened her mouth and attempted to resuscitate her. 'Breathe, Amy....breath!'

***

As she tugged impatiently at the load of dirty clothes squashed into the laundry basket, Abigail mentally listed all the chores she would need to complete that day. She bundled the washing up in her arms and walked into the scullery. Dumping the clothes onto the floor, she began to rifle through the pockets of her husband's trousers. On many occasions she had washed them and later discovered crumpled notes of money, or important business cards clumped in a soggy mess at the bottom of his pockets. She dug deep into the back pocket of his jeans until her fingers located a few coins and a piece of paper. Her stomach lurched as she read the elegant cursive handwriting on the paper. *See you later, darling....*

She read it again. Surely there was a logical explanation? The knot in the pit of her stomach told her otherwise. This woman was intimately involved enough to refer to her husband as *darling*. There was only one possible explanation.

The rest of the day passed in a fog of nervous tension and unbridled anger. There was no doubt he was having an affair. She was surprised he had been so stupid as to leave the woman's card in his pocket. When she thought about it, she considered that he had been distracted and aloof for weeks. The sudden change in his choice of clothes had disturbed her for some time. Eventually she had made peace with her misgivings by putting it down to her husband experiencing a mid-life crisis. He was due to turn fifty in a few months' time.

But why would he leave the piece of paper in his pocket? It just did not make sense. Richard was a cautious and intelligent man.

If indeed he was having an affair, surely, he would cover his tracks more carefully? Perhaps he was hoping to be caught? The thought flittered and darted around her mind like an annoying fly. She tried to imagine what sort of woman she was. A lot could be read through her bold, sophisticated handwriting. It exuded confidence and was almost brazen in the audacious way the message was scribbled on the piece of paper.

Benjamin, her toddler son had been fussy and demanding all day. At two years old, he was the younger of her two children. Her daughter Sophie had just celebrated her fifth birthday. Thankfully, Sophie sat at the coffee table colouring in her book of Walt Disney characters. Barney, the purple dinosaur bellowed from the television. *If you are happy and you know it clap your hands....*

Beyond exhausted from wrestling with a myriad of conflicting emotions, she sighed and flopped into the nearest chair. Now she would just have to wait for her husband's return. There was no doubt in her mind that her next course of action would be to confront him. How would he react? Would he admit he was having an affair, or would he lie to her?

She was alerted to her husband's return through the crunch of his car tyres on the gravel outside. Checking her reflection in the mirror she noticed how tired and drawn she looked. Dark, disillusioned shadows formed half-moons under her eyes. Reaching for her handbag she pulled out her make-up and attempted to cover the evidence of her devastation. The sound of a door slamming pulled her from her thoughts. With slow determination mirrored in her steps she approached the tall figure unbuttoning his coat.

'Hi love, how was your day?' Richard took a step towards her and planted a kiss on her lips. 'Are you OK? You look a little tired.'

'Yes, I am tired. Benjamin has been crabby all day and I've had a stubborn migraine that I can't seem to shake.'

He pulled her into an embrace and tenderly kissed the top of her head. 'Sorry to hear that, darling. Would you like me to make you a cup of tea and then run you a hot bath?'

'No, I still need to get dinner ready. Relax, put your feet up and I will bring you a cup of tea.' Abigail replied with weariness lacing her words. She turned and walked towards the kitchen. Her shattered dreams collected at her feet like the shards of a broken mirror.

***

The fire could not be abated. It was all consuming and insatiable. Diane had kept it at bay for long enough, but the flicker which danced and simmered had found substance to feed upon. It was uncontrollable and could not be contained. Its very nature was wild and unreasonable. The hounds were baying for blood and she could no longer silence them.

Diane wondered when the spark had been ignited. Had the fire always been there, or had it been born out of some dramatic, cataclysmic point in her life? She was aware she was on a journey of self-discovery, which she had not intentionally embarked upon. She was being drawn into a vortex of mixed emotions and roller-coaster extremes. Her desire for security and safety was polarised by an overwhelming need for reckless abandon and wild spontaneity. She realised that turning forty would bring with it a natural contradiction and ambivalence. The distinctive yearning to recapture her youth would have to bow graciously to embrace the inevitable passing of time and all it brought with it. Already, she felt a hand reaching out and pulling her into the dread of middle age.

In a single gulp, she drained the remnants of her tea and drifted outside into the garden. This was her sanctuary and her sanity. It was a quiet, safe place where she could freely vent her internal angst and anger; without feeling any guilt. She yanked at an unsuspecting weed which threatened to choke the life out of her carefully cultivated seedlings. Tugging hard on it to ensure she had removed it from the soil roots and all, she tossed it to the ground at her feet. So much satisfaction derived out of this one seemingly small victory. It allowed her a miniscule sense of achievement, which momentarily restored the power she felt she had lost.

She was fully aware that this would be a time for intense reflection and contemplation. How she had made it this far through the maze of her complicated life she was not entirely sure. A gnawing awareness told her, that to survive her current state of mind and apparent 'mid-life crisis' she would need to find some sense of closure in reaching this magnanimous milestone. Instead, she felt as if a ball and chain was tied around her ankle, anchoring her to the frustration and desperation of her current circumstances and inner turmoil. Where had her aspirations gone? They had taken flight many years ago. Like an audience expecting a better show than offered, her dreams had turned their backs on her in disgust. For years she had been forced to stare into the terrifying abyss of madness. The madness had killed her dreams. She had inherited it like an insidious black cloak that never really fitted. It suffocated her goals and aspirations and ultimately led to her descent into the putrid cesspool of insanity. The black dog of depression stalked her day and night, stealing each last vestige of peace.

Looking back over those years she realised with crystal clear clarity that her life had been a series of obstacles and challenges she had been ill equipped to deal with. Diane resolved she would not allow herself to be dragged into the quagmire of self-pity and regret.

Her frightening world was not a tangible one that surrounded her, but an inner world filled with bitter regret.

She swallowed another pain killer and hoped that it would help to abate her throbbing headache. Perhaps another visit to the Chiropractor would help to ease the hammering in her head.

Diane shrugged on her thick coat and then slammed the front door behind her. Unfortunately, she did not work just around the corner. Although it was quite a distance, it gave her the time and space alone to try to sort through her muddled and disturbing thoughts. There was so much internal conflict going on, that at times she felt she might burst with the frustration of it all. She considered seeing a therapist. But Diane did not have much faith in counsellors and believed them to be human vultures that grew fat on the carcass of human suffering. There would also be plenty for them to feed on as life in general was becoming increasingly stressful as time marched on.

She wondered if this was a collective state or whether she was the only one living in this state of mind. There must be hundreds, maybe thousands of women out there who were battling with the same issues. The problem was society imposed so much pressure to always keep up the appearance of happiness. Anyone who was depressed was seen to be a nuisance. Perhaps, they believed the threat of bursting the bubble of denial was so huge that they chose to squash it. Stamp out all questioning thoughts, deny, deny, deny. It was so much easier that way.

If she could at least unravel some of her thoughts and frustrations she could find a way through the maze. The darkness suffocated her, and she longed for the light. It was the emotional roller-coaster ride that she found so exhausting. At times she felt like she was in heaven and at other times it was pure hell. She found herself wondering if it was the circumstances of her life or the thoughts in her head that were causing the turmoil and dissatisfaction.

It is ironic and mildly amusing she found herself thinking. Her life appeared picture perfect from the outside. She was married to a handsome, kind and intelligent man and her career was thriving. She had climbed the corporate ladder and was now a partner in a prestigious law firm. The only dark stain on her otherwise rosy life was the fact that she had never been able to bear children.

The traffic was slow and tedious. Like wading through mud, but at least it gave her time to lose herself in her thoughts. Diane enjoyed the long drive to work as it was entirely her time. She could switch off and not have to concern herself with the demands of home. Her thoughts began to wonder into the complex political maze that she would have to carefully navigate once she arrived at her office. She was bombarded by the tasks of the day that lay ahead and the diplomacy she would need to manage her colleagues.

Diane knew her work had begun to consume her. The situation would have to change. She could not continue living like this, but she was not entirely sure how she would implement that change. Financially she was not able to give up her job. Especially because of the current economic climate of doom and gloom. She was not sure she was brave enough to chance leaving her job.

Her thoughts turned towards the man who dominated her every waking thought. Guilt snaked through her like a serpent concealed by the long grass of her tortured mind. She had fallen just twice and yet it was all it had taken to burst into flame her long suppressed desires. Her husband, Jeremy had not touched her in months. He was so consumed with his job that he barely noticed how far she had withdrawn into her shell. Images of her new lover's face appeared before her eyes. He made her feel so invigorated and young again. But guilt was knocking like a stranger at the door to her heart.

Never had there been a reason to feel such gut-wrenching guilt. If she felt so guilty then why was it so hard to stop thinking about him?

***

The jelly smeared across her bare stomach in preparation for the ultrasound scan felt cold and uncomfortable. Tiffany squirmed in irritation. But as soon as she heard the baby's heartbeat, something in the depths of her being was awakened. Had she in fact made the right decision or was she going to regret it for the rest of her life? As she wrestled with her emotions, Jason's face suddenly appeared before her. She loved him desperately and without his support there was no way she had the strength to bring a child into the world alone. Covering her ears, she sat up and reached for a tissue. Her mind began to wander back to the day she had found out she was pregnant.

When she confronted Jason with the news, her cheeks had been flushed with excitement. After living with him for over a year, she truly believed he would marry her someday.

'Jason, I have some news for you.' Tiffany said tentatively. She sat down on the couch next to him and took his hand. Inhaling, she looked deep into his eyes.

'I'm pregnant.' The silence that stretched between them was fraught with tension. Like an acrobat on a tightrope.

'Please say something, Jason. I know it is unexpected!'

Tiffany watched his jaw muscles twitch in frustration. He clenched his fists and stood up.

'How could you be so stupid? I thought you were on the pill!' Jason's tone was hostile and cold. You are only twenty years old! There is no way you are ready to raise a child and besides....'

'What, Jason? This has more to do with you than it does with me. Just admit it, you don't want this baby.'

He began to pace the length of the room.

'I am not going to lie to you. Of course, I do not want to have a child. It is not exactly on my agenda, there is still so much I want to do with my life. I suppose you have delusions about settling down and getting married. Sorry Tiffany, it's just not what I want at this stage in my life.'

'Well, there's nothing more to say. What do you expect me to do now?' Tiffany's lip began to quiver as she struggled to suppress her tears. 'Do you think I planned this, Jason? I know I am not ready for a child. But how can you blame this on me? I have been using contraception, but I have also been sick lately. Maybe the anti-biotic I have been taking has had an effect. I don't know....'

'Well, it's too late now, isn't it? There is no use crying over spilt milk. You are just going to have to get rid of it. That is the only solution. How can you put me in this position, Tiffany?'

'How can you say that? I cannot believe you are being so cruel! I don't want to get rid of it, Jason.'

Acid contempt dripped off his tongue as he turned to look at her. 'You had better have an abortion, Tiffany. If you do not, you and I are over. You can kiss our future goodbye. Maybe in a few years once we are married, we can have a child.'

Tiffany began to cry, her tears forming tiny rivers down her cheeks. 'I don't want to lose you…'

'Well then, if you don't want me to leave then you had better go ahead and make a plan.'

The enormity of the decision she would have to make weighed heavily on her shoulders. She could not believe that he was asking her to choose. Jason was the love of her life. The first man she had ever been with and she hoped he would be the last. Perhaps he was right. They were both unprepared and maybe if she waited a few years they could have a child once they were married. By then they would be ready. And, what would her parents say? They would be so ashamed of her. She had been raised in a Catholic home and having a child out of wedlock would be the ultimate sin in their eyes. If she had an abortion, they would never know she was pregnant.

'Fine, I will look into it.' She said with a resigned sigh. 'I have a friend at work who recently had the procedure done. I am sure she will give me the phone number of the clinic.'

'That's my girl.' Pulling her to her feet, Jason cupped her face in his hands. 'You are doing the right thing. It may not seem like it now, but one day you will look back and it will all make sense. You know that I love you, right?'

She nuzzled her head into his neck and inhaled the aftershave he was wearing. The familiar scent warmed her. Everything would be fine she was certain of it. The horrific reality of what she was about to do was pushed to the back of her mind.

The following morning, she waited for a quiet moment at work so she could make an inquiry about the clinic. She cornered Natasha in the kitchen whilst she was making a cup of tea.

'Natasha, I need to speak to you about something. It is personal so can you have to promise me that you will keep it strictly confidential. Please... you can't tell anyone.'

'Sure, Tiff. What is it?'

'I need the telephone number of the clinic you went to a few weeks ago.' A long pause, pregnant with questions hung between them for a few seconds. Natasha searched Tiffany's eyes.

'Are you sure it's the route you want to go. They do not just do it, you know. They will interview you to establish exactly why you can't have the baby…'

'Yes, I have given it lots of thought. I am far too young to have a child and besides, Jason told me to do it.'

Natasha sucked in a sharp breath. 'Wow, that's a bit heavy. How do you feel about him putting the pressure on you?'

'At first, I was a little taken aback but now that I think about it, I can see his point. He feels he is too young to settle down. His career is foremost in his mind right now and we can always have another child once we are married.'

'If you are really sure it's what you want then I will get you the phone number. But maybe you should give it a few more days. Once it is done, there is no going back. Who else knows about this? Have you told your parents?'

'No! They are the last people I could tell. Mum and Dad would be horrified. I am sure they would never forgive me and would feel like I have shamed the family. They must never know.'

'It's a really big decision to make on your own.'

'I know, but it's not like I am alone in all of this. I have Jason and he will be supportive I am sure.'

Natasha continued to stare at Tiffany. An uneasy feeling had settled in the pit of her stomach.

She was not sure she wanted to be pulled into this mess. If ever Tiffany regretted her decision, she would feel responsible. But it was not her decision, so she decided that if Tiffany had her mind set on it, she was prepared to help.

'Meet me at the pub downstairs after work and I will give you the number then. You will probably need a stiff drink. If you are anything like me, you must be feeling pretty frightened right now.'

***

Patrick had begun to snore as Charlotte sat under the kitchen table biding her time. She needed to be sure he was sound asleep so she could creep out undetected. Loosening her grip on the butcher's knife in her hand, she closed her eyes and sighed. Surely, she had lost her mind! What kind of woman plots to murder her husband? But the years of immeasurable abuse had taken their toll. The innocent, trusting and naive woman she used to be had long ago died. All that was left was a tortured and lost soul who was drowning in a sea of despair and fear.

She crawled out from beneath the table and stood next to her husband. His face was squashed into the table and spit drooled from his mouth. Where was the handsome, charming man she had once known? When she first met him, he had seemed so well balanced. But she had been so young and trusting. On a warm, summer's day her friends had invited her to a picnic in a park nearby. Little had she known that a single encounter with a stranger would set her on a path which would lead to heartache and destruction? Even her friends had been taken in by him. There were no signs. No red flags or warning bells. She could kick herself now, as could her friend who had introduced them. All she had seen back then was the passionate medical student who had high ambitions for his life and endless affection for her. He was an astute and gifted surgeon respected by many by day. But come nightfall and a few rounds of alcohol and he became a monster.

Charlotte walked over to the kitchen counter and opened the top drawer. She carefully placed the butcher's knife into it and closed the drawer. Turning around, she leaned against the counter and started to cry. Gut wrenching sobs began to tremble inside her. With one last look at her husband she walked out of the room and down the passage. Desperate for some fresh air, she walked outside and lifted her face to the bright sunshine. Again, she considered her options. Would it be possible to leave him? She longed to be free. The thought of flying high above the constrictions and torment of her life thrilled her. Instinctively she knew he would hunt her down. His obsession with her was unrelenting.

The beginnings of a throbbing headache knocked inside her skull like a jackhammer. She turned to walk inside. As she stepped into the doorway, she saw a pile of letters had been shoved through her post box. Rifling through them she noticed a brightly coloured leaflet. She began to read it.

Are you lonely and broken? Have your dreams been shattered through life's hurts? Come and join the Apples of Gold support group. Here you will find experienced Christian counsellors who would like to help you. Meetings take place the first Thursday evening of every month at seven o'clock in Pitshanger Lane Town Hall.

Could this be what she was looking for? A place where she could meet other women suffering in similar circumstances to her own? She had mixed feelings. By nature, she was a deeply private person who believed it to be wrong to air her dirty laundry in public.

Charlotte read it again. Hope ignited within her. Maybe, this was exactly what she needed. She folded the paper in half and shoved it in her pocket. Patrick must not catch wind of it, or he would try to stop her from attending the meetings. Stepping through the door she closed it behind her and walked towards her bedroom at the end of the hall. There was bound to be a few headache tablets left in her bathroom cabinet. Arriving there she stood at the basin and stared into the mirror. She was only thirty-nine and yet she looked years older. The lines around her eyes had deepened and the glimmer that used to dance in her eyes had faded. Now they appeared sunken and vacuous.

She reached for the bottle of painkillers in the cabinet and quickly swallowed two of the tablets. Perhaps if she lay down in a darkened room, she would be able to shake the headache.

Charlotte was woken from her brief sleep by the sound of banging dishes. Patrick had obviously risen from his drunken stupor. A shiver of dread shot through her. Now his mood would be worst than ever. He would be nursing a hangover and angry that his dinner had not been prepared. As if on cue, he began to yell.

'Charlotte…' he called with an indignant edge to his voice. 'What the hell have you been doing all afternoon?' There was petulance in his footsteps as he stomped up the stairs. He stood in the doorway glaring at her. She sat up rubbing the sleep from her eyes.

'I was tired, Patrick so I just took a short nap.'

'What on earth are you tired from? What do you do all day? I am the one who goes out there every day trying to bring home the bacon. The least you can do is prepare something to eat.'

Charlotte was grateful that even though he was belligerent and nasty, he was not drunk. If he had been, she would have received a beating by now. Even so, she was not going to take the risk of incurring his wrath again.

She sat up and inched her toes into her flannel slippers. Where had her life gone, she wondered? Hours of her time were spent thinking about the kind of life she should be living. In her dreams she was married to a kind, loving man who doted on her. She was sure that if she were involved with a man like that, she would be blissfully happy. He would be a caring family man and they would be surrounded by children. She was the only child. The product of a brief, unhappy union and as a result she longed to have four of her own babies. The miscarriage had knocked the life out of her.

Every day her arms longed to hold her child. Her dreams were filled with the sound of a crying baby. In the nightmare she could never reach her child. She would run and run but the pitch-black darkness surrounding her sucked the breath out of her and she would collapse gasping. The cries of the child would grow louder and louder until eventually she would clap her hands over her ears and sob in agony.

***

Abigail stood at the kitchen counter waiting for the kettle to boil. She weighed her options carefully. Should she confront Richard with his infidelity, or would it be better to wait until she had more proof? If she did ask him, would he confess everything or concoct a lie? Somehow, she had lost sight of who he truly was. Had she ever really known him? The man she loved had disappeared the moment she had first set eyes on the words which pierced her heart.

*See you later; darling...*Like a cat toying with a mouse, the words tormented her. They taunted her to believe that her husband of ten years was in love with another woman. The single line of writing seemed so intimate. Her mind tried to find a logical explanation for why he should be carrying that piece of paper. But there was only one reason and she would have to face the truth. Richard was having an affair.

After pouring the tea, she turned and walked towards the lounge. Her chest hurt and her hands shook slightly as she put the cup on the table next to him. She would have to find out the truth. There was no other way. Denial was not an option and if she tried to ignore her emotions, they would betray her. He would be able to read the questions in her eyes. She sat down and tried to straighten out the creases in her skirt. Suddenly the room felt thick with tension as the walls closed in on her.

She turned towards him, trembling inwardly as she braced herself.

'Richard, I need to ask you something.' Shoving her hand into her pocket, she fingered the piece of paper and waited for him to focus his attention on her. Finally, he drained his cup and looked at her. As she handed the paper to him, she searched his face for a clue.

His voice rose as he asked her a question. 'Where did you get this?' His tone was accusatory.

'I found it in your trouser pocket when I was doing the washing. Richard, I think I should be the one asking the questions, don't you?'

His eyes darted around the room. 'Do you think I am having an affair?' He asked, his voice rising in alarm.

'Well yes. It certainly seems that way. Who is she?'

'A client I met a week ago. She is doing some work for a project. I barely know her. I wouldn't make too much of it...she calls everyone darling!'

'Do you honestly expect me to believe you? Surely you can understand how ridiculous your explanation sounds?'

'Abigail, you can believe me or not. But I swear I am telling the truth. What more do you want me to say? I cannot admit to something that isn't going on.' He stood up and glared at her. 'I really don't have the time for this. I am going to take a shower.' Richard turned and marched out of the room. His indignation trailed behind him like tendrils of smoke. She stood up and reached for the empty cups. Her mind wrestled with his explanation. Could it be that he was telling the truth? Should she believe him? Deep inside she desperately wanted to. But her gut told her otherwise. He was lying; there was no doubt about it.

Her pride refused to allow him to see how much she was hurting. There was only one course of action now. She would have to wait until she had more proof and then confront him with the evidence. In future, she would watch him carefully. But it was likely he would cover his tracks with caution. One day, he would slip up and then she would catch him out. The anger started to writhe within. She needed to vent it somehow. A workout at the gym would most likely do the trick. She bounded up the stairs and entered her bedroom. The water was gushing out of the shower as Richard lathered his body with soap. She popped her head around the door.

'I'm going to the gym. Dinner is in the oven if you're hungry,' she said trying hard to suppress the pain in her voice.

'I'll see you later. Enjoy yourself.'

Abigail clenched her teeth in irritation. It was inconceivable how he could blatantly lie to her with such ease. Did he not have a conscience? Who was this man and what had happened to her once happy marriage? She had always believed that they would be immune to infidelity. On countless occasions she had begged him to never ever betray her. His answer was always the same. 'I love you Abigail and I would never do that to you.' The words sickened her.

She threw on her gym clothes and left the house. Jumping into her car, she checked the rear-view mirror and then pulled out of the driveway impatiently. As she drove down the freeway her mind raced. What was she going to do now? It would be near impossible to hide her belief that he was lying to her. It would take all strength to appear as if everything were normal.

The thought of a divorce terrified her. Her parents had split when she was very young. Her father had been unfaithful, and her mother had immediately called for a break-up of the marriage. Abigail was devastated and never truly got over the trauma. For many years she hoped and prayed that her parents would reconcile but they never did. Both parties remarried. There was no way she was going to put her children through the same suffering she endured. If it was at all possible, she was determined to save her marriage. If only Richard would admit to his infidelity. If he was truly sorry, she might consider forgiving him. The thought occurred to her that maybe he was in love with the woman. What if he left her?

Abigail's best friend Sarah came to mind. She had found out that her husband had been unfaithful to her less than six months ago. A bitter divorce had ensued, and the custody battle had been ugly and brutal. Both of her children were deeply hurt by the fiasco and although they remained with their mother, they constantly yearned for their father to return. Sarah had just started taking them to a child psychologist to help them process the pain they were experiencing.

The gym was packed tighter than a bus full of tourists. Abigail swiped her card at the entrance and then hurried to the nearest treadmill. The angst inside of her was begging to be released and she was eager to run from her troubles. She cranked up the speed to as fast as she could tolerate and then ran as if the devil himself was chasing her.

***

It had been a long, stressful day and Diane was longing to leave the office. She finished checking her emails and then logged off her computer. She smiled at the thought of the evening ahead. She was due to meet her lover. The thrill of seeing him again was peppered with guilt. Her illicit affair had only just begun but she knew she needed to end it.

A chance meeting at a work function sparked a mutual interest which burned like an uncontrollable fire. Fueled by an insatiable passion and hungry desire. They met a second time at a conference the following week. After a few too many glasses of wine, the inevitable happened and they ended up in bed together. David was everything she longed for in a man. Handsome, cultured and intelligent...the list was endless. Her marriage had felt stagnant for years.

The ache that longed for newness, something different and life altering was as palpable as sour drops of lemon on her tongue. The fond familiarity of her marriage had once embraced her like an old sofa, but complacency had shuffled in and squeezed in next to her. Suddenly, she felt suffocated.

On the odd occasion, she enjoyed her husband's company. At a stretch it could be mistaken for a long-forgotten love. But on this icy winter's afternoon, Diane shivered at the thought of spending time with her husband. She had told him she was attending a work function and would be home very late.

She rang the buzzer of the apartment building where David lived and waited for him to let her in. The sound of his voice over the intercom immediately warmed her.

'Hi David, it's me.'

'Come in.'

Within seconds she was standing at his front door, a hard knot formed in her stomach. He opened the door before she had a chance to knock.

'I wasn't sure you would make it, Diane. It really is great to see you.' He stepped aside allowing her to pass. 'Can I get you a drink? If your day has been anything like mine, I am sure you will want one.'

'Yes, please.' Diane said, perching herself on the edge of the sofa.

'What would you like? I've got a bottle of Cabernet Sauvignon if you are interested.'

'That sounds wonderful, David.' Nervously biting her lip, she wondered what on earth she was doing there. Torn between wanting to stay and the desire to run, she found herself rooted to the spot.

'There you go,' he said handing her a glass of wine.

'That's lovely, thank you.' She sipped from it unable to meet his eyes.

'Diane, are you alright? You look a little pale.'

'I'm fine. Just a little unsure about what I am doing here. I really should be going.'

'But you've only just arrived. What is bothering you? Would you like to talk about it?'

'Well it's just, you know...'

'Yes, we shouldn't be doing this. You have your family, I have mine.' David said reading her thoughts.

'Exactly! I couldn't have said it better myself.'

'I hear you, Diane. But let us think carefully about this. We cannot deny that there is something special between us. We both knew it from the moment we met. If you were happily married, then maybe we would need to stop it right here. But you told me about your husband. It sounds to me like he does not appreciate you. When is the last time he told you he loves you? You deserve better than that.'

'I can't remember when he last said those words to me. Even so, what we are doing is wrong. We both made vows. I know you said your wife was unfaithful, but it was your choice to stay with her. We should stop this now and work on our marriages.' Diane looked down at her hands and sighed.

'I know that from a moral point of view what we are doing is wrong, but we didn't exactly plan this. It just happened. Stop beating yourself up, Diane. If you are so unhappy with your husband, why don't you just divorce him?'

'I have thought long and hard about it, David. I cannot leave him now. He would be devastated.'

'You have a right to be happy. I am falling in love with you and perhaps we have a future together?'

Diane looked at David, warmed by the tenderness she saw on his face. 'I feel the same way,' she said sadly. What are we going to do?'

'For now, we can just enjoy being together. How can it be wrong when we are so comfortable with each other? I feel as if I have known you forever. I wish you had come into my life a long time ago.' David pulled Diane into his arms.

'My husband is a good man and he doesn't deserve this. I am not sure I will ever stop feeling guilty,' Diane said pulling away from him.

David stroked her face. 'Do you want to end this?'

She looked down at her trembling hands. 'I am not sure I have the strength to do that. It is so long since I felt so alive. I realise I have been dead inside for so long now.'

'I understand what you are saying. My wife and I have led different lives for years now. Sometime the loneliness is more than I can bear. I feel such a strong connection with you.'

'Maybe we should try with our spouses one more time?' Diane asked tentatively.

'We have had copious sessions of counselling and I have been trying to repair the damage for years. To be honest, I think she is preparing herself for a divorce. I wouldn't be surprised if she were seeing someone else as well.'

'My husband would never have an affair. I have never had reason to doubt him. That's what makes this situation so difficult.'

'Diane, do you want to try and reconcile with your husband?'

'I'm just not sure. Maybe I should put a little distance between us and give it some thought. I'm sorry, but I really must be going.'

'I can't say I am not sorry but if you feel that you have to go then I will just have to respect that.'

Diane reached for her car keys resting on the coffee table and stood to leave. 'I'm sorry, David. I should never have got involved with you in the first place.' He nodded and looked away. It tore his heart out hearing her say those words but in the depths of his being he knew she was right. It would be different if they were both divorced.

'Goodbye Diane,' he said softly.

It occurred to her that if she was indeed making the right choice then why did it feel so wrong?

Whilst driving home she was bombarded with an army of conflicting thoughts. Like mist rolling in over the sea, discontent had settled over her. It was cloying and seemed to nestle deep in her bones. Realistically, she had no reason to be dissatisfied. She had a kind, doting husband and a flourishing career. They were certainly comfortable financially. It galled her that she had the nerve to not be content in her circumstances. But the pervading thought that she hated her life seemed to follow her around like a stray dog.

***

The tiny white casket at the front of the church appeared tragically out of place in the huge room. Jessica laid a wreath of pink roses on the top and then took her seat on the closest pew. Numb with grief, she could barely function, let alone speak at her daughter's funeral. Like a coastal town stripped bare by a tsunami, she felt naked and raw with emotion. Today, her eyes were dry and devoid of tears. Days of weeping had left her spent and broken. Getting out of bed on this terrible day had been harder than she could ever have imagined.

The enormity of her devastation engulfed her. Since hearing the news of Amy's drowning only four days ago, she had operated on auto pilot. Losing her beautiful child had sucked the life out of her. She felt like a pricked balloon slowly, painfully deflating as the life drained out of her. Going through the motions like a mechanical engine was the only way she could put one foot in front of the other. Nothing would bring her darling child back to her. There was no use dwelling on *what ifs*, and *if onlys.*

Craig blamed himself for their child's death. On that fateful day, he was supposed to be baby-sitting and instead he had chosen to watch a game of rugby on the television. Foolishly, he had given the responsibility to his stepdaughter. Not only had Bethany failed to keep a careful eye on Amy, but she had also not checked to ensure the child's water wings were adequately inflated. This error had cost the little girl her life.

Surprisingly, Jessica did not blame her husband or her daughter. She blamed herself. It was a mother's job to always be there for her children. To protect and nurture no matter what it cost. In her mind, she had let Amy down. Even though she had simply popped out to the shop for twenty minutes, her child should have accompanied her.

As the organ music began to play a hymn, images from Amy's short life began to flash before Jessica's eyes. The day she was born, her first step...her first word. Memories marched across her mind forming a rich kaleidoscope of images. She remembered Amy walking through the gates at her pre-school. As Jessica blew a kiss to her, she would jump and catch it. Then she would solemnly clutch it to her heart, her chubby fist clenched protectively over her treasure. 'Got you in my heart,' she would yell. Gently, the wind would catch the words and deliver them to her mother with a gentle sigh.

Amy had been the product of her second marriage and the ultimate love child. Jessica had been amazed that at the ripe age of forty-one she had managed to conceive. Amy was a welcome surprise and much needed sibling for her elder sister. Despite the large age gap of eleven years, Bethany doted on her little sister. The fact that she now blamed herself for Amy's death only added to the tragedy. At the age of fourteen she was battling enough internal angst without the added pressure of self-loathing and regret.

Jessica knew the time would come for her to take her eldest daughter to a therapist. She needed help to work through the maze of torment she was suffering. But for now, Jessica barely had the strength to make it through Amy's memorial service. Her other daughter's needs were the farthest from her mind.

St Mary's Church was swollen with grief-stricken members of the local community. All present acknowledged that there had always been something special about Amy. A light had shone within her and easily captivated every person she met. Possessing wisdom beyond her years, she was an old soul in the body of a four-year old. Somehow, her little blue eyes had a penetrating knowing that softened even the hardest heart. Even the reclusive old man who lived at the end of her street had walked into the church to pay his respects.

A single encounter with Amy had touched his life forever. On a warm, sunny afternoon he had visited the store at the same time as Jessica and Amy. He was paying for a loaf of bread and carton of milk. As it was the end of the month, his pension money was stretched to the limit and failed to cover the expense of his groceries. Amy had overheard the conversation between the cashier and Mr Jones.

'I'm sorry; Sir... but you don't have enough for both the items. Perhaps you would like to choose one?' The man had huffed and puffed and muttered something about the ridiculous price of things. Amy tugged on her mother's sleeve to gain her attention.

'Please help him, Mummy. Otherwise he won't be able to have a cup of tea.' Jessica smiled and paid the balance. Mr Jones nodded gratefully and left the store leaning heavily on his cane.

Often, those who knew and loved Amy had remarked on her sensitivity towards the needs of others. Her heart was the size of Africa and often she talked about how she wanted to help orphaned children when she grew up. She could read the emotions of the children around her and was always the first to comfort a crying child. Her classmates loved her dearly. Her popularity was evident through the numerous parties and play dates she was invited to.

A fresh flood of tears began to tremble in Jessica's eyes. How on earth was she going to get over losing her angelic child? Where was God at a time like this? Her faith had always been strong but now it wavered like a candle flickering in the wind. This travesty was bound to snuff it out. It was inconceivable that a loving heavenly Father could allow such suffering into her life. Hadn't she served him since her teenage years? She had even worked as one of the leaders of the youth group at her church. Why had her Lord abandoned her?

There were those who had said that *heaven had gained an angel.* These trite words seared through her like a hot poker and only served to intensify the pain. She did not want God to take her precious child. Jessica needed her little girl more than God did. The hole in her heart screamed to be filled with the sound of her baby's voice. How could people be so insensitive? Although she knew they were trying to comfort her, their condolences had done nothing but add to her loneliness and despair.

Craig felt a million miles away from her. He was not able to reach her. She was trapped in a tomb of remorse and self-loathing. A single record played repeatedly in her mind. *This is your fault. You should have been there.*

***

Jason accompanied Tiffany to the clinic. Internally, he was wrestling with his decision. Was it the right one? Was it fair of him to force her into an abortion? But the more he thought about it, the greater his resolve grew. He told himself that she was not ready to raise a child, but the truth was he was the one who was not ready. The thought that he was being selfish never occurred to him.

He had been waiting patiently to see Tiffany for the past couple of hours. The doctor had informed him that it would only take an hour for the procedure and then she would be sent to the recovery ward. Surely, she must have woken from the anesthetic by now. He walked over to the receptionist. 'Please could you find out if I can see my girlfriend now?'

'Certainly, sir. What is her name?'

'Tiffany Rogers.'

She got up and walked through a door into another room. Jason could hear muffled voices on the other side of the door. Within minutes she re-entered the room.

'Yes, you can go and see her now. Follow me, please.'

Jason walked over to Tiffany's bedside. She was curled onto her side in the fetal position, her eyes closed.

'How are you, Tiff?' He said stroking the hair from her face. She turned towards him her voice groggy.

'I've been better, Jason.' She said softly. He sat in the chair beside her bed and reached for her hand.

'It is for the best....'

'I know, you keep telling me that, but I feel a mixture of relief and regret.'

'I am sure that it's understandable, Tiff. We must just give it time and I am sure you will eventually get over this. Just keep focusing on our future and the child we are going to have once we're married.'

'Yes, I suppose you're right. It is just that I feel as if there is a gaping hole inside of me. It was so awful Jason.

Before I went in for the operation, they did an ultra-sound. I heard the heartbeat...'

Jason inhaled and then breathed out slowly as he collected his thoughts. He was not expecting this latest piece of information. He had read the pro-life leaflet. It said nothing in there about an ultra-sound scan.

'I don't know what to say, my angel. How did you feel when you heard it?'

'What do you think I felt, Jason? Confused, scared, unsure about whether we had made the right choice. Maybe I should have hung on. Had the child and then put it up for adoption.'

'Let us just look ahead now. In time, you will forget about this ordeal. We'll just take it one day at a time…'

'Jason, it was so awful in the recovery ward. There must have been about a dozen girls in there. They were all very young. One of them looked about fourteen years old. The look on their faces will haunt me forever. I felt like we were cattle being herded through the slaughter-house.'

Desperate to change the subject, Jason interrupted her.

'Tiff. I do not want to talk about it anymore. Let us just focus on the positive. When can I get you out of here?'

'The doctor said I can go as soon as I've have recovered from the surgery. I feel fine and would like to leave as soon as possible.'

'Are you feeling any pain?' He asked with clear concern woven into his voice.

'There is a dull ache. Almost like a period cramp but other than that I feel fine. The doctor said I will bleed for a few days.'

'Let us get you out of here then. Get dressed and I will go and sign the release papers.'

Tiffany grimaced as she sat up. A ball of fire ignited in her womb. She reached for the pain killers the doctor had prescribed. Getting up slowly she padded softly over to the basin and filled a glass with water. She swallowed the pills and then reached for her duffel bag. Perhaps the familiarity of her clothes would help her feel better. She pulled on her tracksuit and then sat down on the bed. Somehow, she had been expecting to feel differently after the operation. Instead she felt hollow and empty. She inhaled sharply and blinked back the tears. It was best that she focused on what Jason had said to her. Their future was bright with possibility. The day would come when she would hold a baby in her arms. This surreal feeling that seemed to permeate her bones was probably a side effect of the operation. Once she was home and she had the chance to continue with her life, everything would be fine.

Jason walked into the room and smiled.

'Let us get going.' Pulling her into his arms, he squeezed her tight. 'Try not to think about it too much. It will only depress you, my darling.'

Tiffany nodded against his chest. She always felt so safe in his arms. He stooped to pick up her bag and then grabbed her hand tugging her gently. Determined to escape from the reality of the situation, they walked quickly through the clinic doors into another grey, rainy day.

They raced down the steps towards the London underground. It was rush hour and already the commuters were swarming around like bees in a hive. They managed to get on the train just as the doors were about to close. As she studied the faces surrounding her, Tiffany was struck by the thought that for most people, it was just another day. It was likely that nothing extra ordinary had happened for them on this day. They had woken up, got dressed, caught the train, worked another full day and were now on their way home to their uneventful lives.

But no matter how much she tried to convince herself nothing life changing or significant had happened, deep within her she knew she had made the biggest mistake of her life. Without thinking it through properly, she had recklessly taken a child's life. The guilt that knew no mercy would hound her for the rest of her days.

Although Jason had pushed her to carry out the sinister act, it had been her decision to follow through. He was not to blame for taking the life of an innocent child. It was her fault....

***

For the second time that day, Diane considered coming clean about her affair. But Jeremy would be devastated and would most likely ask for a divorce. There was no way Diane could sabotage her future. Besides, she still loved Jeremy and he certainly did not deserve to be hurt after everything he had done for her. The marriage had withered and died like a plant starved of water and sunshine. Somehow the closeness they once shared was gone and Diane was not sure how she could get it back.

In the back of her mind a warning bell was sounding. She believed she had incurring the wrath of God and His judgement was upon her. She struggled with the concept of God being a loving father who would extend grace and mercy towards her should she repent of her sin. Having grown up with a harsh, dictatorial father who ridiculed her constantly, she could not possibly relate to a gracious heavenly father. For years, her mother had tried to convert her father to the Christian faith, but it was futile. He was an atheist by nature and her words fell on deaf ears. Diane had watched her mother fervently follow her Saviour but had also seen how it did not ensure her mother a happy life. Instead she had led a quiet, desperate life filled with tears and regret. She never truly got over the fact that her husband did not share her faith. Then at the age of sixty-five, her mother suddenly developed stomach cancer and was dead within six months.

Whenever Diane thought about the mother she had lost, pools of grief would form in her eyes. She desperately missed her mother's gentle, kind nature. They had shared a strong bond. It was a cord that could not be broken through the storms of life. As a result, Diane was angry at God. How could he take away her precious mother and leave her reeling from shock? A cavernous hole existed within her and no matter how hard she tried nothing could fill it.

Jeremy had been supportive and caring since the day Diane heard the news of her mother's passing. The grief had sliced through her like a knife through warm butter. Never had she felt so lost and adrift. Almost as if her mother had defined who she was. Suddenly she did not know who she was anymore. It was if the rug had been pulled out from beneath her feet. Now, she would have to forge her own path. All her childhood insecurities had surfaced like bubbles of air in the ocean of her despair. She was aware that even though her husband had reached out to her, she had rejected his advances. How could he possibly know how she felt when his own mother was alive and well? Part of her resented him. Although it was wrong, she could not seem to stop herself.

The thought that perhaps she was truly a horrible person began to knock at the door of her heart. Why was she so recklessly endangering her marriage? On a subconscious level did she want out, or was she just acting on a selfish urge that seemed to consume her? No good could possibly come of her affair. The irony was that she had always believed that he would be the one who would be unfaithful. Isn't that what men did? Her father had never seemed to be able to stop himself. Her long-suffering mother had eventually reconciled herself to the fact that her husband would never change.

Diane asked herself why she was having an affair. Was she angry with Jeremy on some unconscious level? He did not deserve to be treated this way. She knew she had pushed him away for years. Intimacy scared her and it was far easier to be involved in a purely physical affair than to truly share her soul with a man. The ghosts of her past still haunted her.

Trapped in an ambivalent vortex, she found sex both satisfying and repulsive. Little did she know that her entire married life would be filled with a roller coaster of extremes as far as her emotions were concerned. It also never occurred to her just how transparent she was. Jeremy was aware that she withdrew from him no matter how much she reassured him. Their intimate life was superficial and hollow. Although it was often satisfying on a physical level, they never truly connected the way a husband and wife should. There was a dark stain on her soul which no man could ever remove. She was chained to her abuser no matter how hard she tried to break free.

Jeremy tried to be patient with Diane but on many occasions the sense that he had lost her overwhelmed him. The fact that she was having an affair would serve as the guillotine which would obliterate their marriage. Diane was fully aware of the fact that her infidelity would break him.

It was so much easier to be intimate with a man she was not in love with. She could withdraw emotionally and remain detached. But she knew the time would come when she would have to face the demons of her past. Her abuse clung to her like a rotting carcass and the burden was becoming increasingly difficult to carry. It was not fair on her husband to continually pull away from him emotionally. He deserved to connect with her on a deep level.

Diane considered that she had to put her fears to bed and rise from the ashes of her pain. The thought flittered around her mind every day.

***

Jessica held Amy's teddy bear to her chest. Her heart constricted in agony as the tears slid down her cheeks. It had been just a month since she had lost her precious baby girl. Yet it seemed like an eternity since she had last held her cherished child. The days stretched before her empty and barren. No longer did her little girl's voice echo through the rooms of her house. An eerie silence had descended on her home. Craig had withdrawn into his shell and was unreachable. His zest for life dimmed like a dying sun dipping into an ocean of despair and guilt. Of course, he blamed himself.

Amy's pink bedroom adorned with stuffed animals and Hello Kitty posters had not been touched since she had died. Jessica did not have the heart to change it. On some days she would sit on her pretty, floral bedspread and hold her flannel nightdress to her nose. But now her baby smell of talcum powder and softly scented soap had faded and all that remained were memories of her laughter. A gentle song, which seemed to dance on the air like a flurry of colourful butterflies. Jessica spread her hand over the pillow and placed the teddy bear in the center.

Sometimes she would close her eyes and imagine holding her baby in her arms. 'Mummy, did you know that Eskimos kiss by rubbing their noses together? Sebastian told me at school.'

Amy had said the words with a serious look on her face. A smile tugged at the corners of her little rosebud mouth as she nodded, her blonde curls bobbing in a golden halo around her head. The memory of that moment sliced through Jessica. She groaned and began to sob. 'My baby, I want you back... I can't stand the pain,' she whispered through ragged breaths.

Her faith in God had been severely shaken through the tragedy. How could a good, kind and loving Heavenly Father allow her cherished child to be snatched away from her? Jessica had grown up in a Christian home and knew that she should believe in God's plan for her life but how could it possibly involve this level of heart ache? Her heart had turned cold on the day she had lost her daughter. Her belief system had been turned upside down and now she was struggling to believe that the Saviour she had walked with for years truly had her best interests at heart. Her favourite scripture suddenly came to mind. *Know the plans I have for you says the Lord. Plans to prosper you and not to harm you, plans to give you a hope and a future....*

What sort of future did she have now that her baby was gone? It took all her courage and will power just to get out of bed in the morning. Putting one foot in front of the other proved to be an enormous task which sucked the energy out of her. If she did not have to drive Bethany to school every day, she would most likely sleep her life away. Only then could she escape the torment. The medication her doctor prescribed lulled her into a deep slumber which brought some reprieve. But of late, she was tormented by nightmares where she could hear Amy calling out to her. But no matter how hard she tried she could never reach her.

She knew the time would come when she would have to move on. Amy's bedroom would need to be packed up and she would have to reconcile herself to the fact that she was never coming back. But she was not ready to let go yet. Her friends were beginning to whisper behind her back. She was aware of their concern. But why could they not understand that she was merely trying to find a way through her grief? The tunnel of heartache was one that she would not easily emerge from and she was not sure that time would heal her either. Perhaps time would ease the sting of her loss but deep in the recesses of her ravaged heart she knew that she would never get over losing her little angel.

Often, she contemplated suicide. It would be so easy to just put an end to it all. She could swallow the entire contents of her sleeping pill bottle and be done with it. The mere idea of sinking into oblivion and never waking up again was incredibly appealing. But she had to remember that she had another child to care for. It would be unthinkably selfish to kill herself and leave Bethany without a mother.

Her thoughts turned towards her teenage daughter. At fourteen she was so impressionable, and she was carrying enormous guilt over what had transpired on that fateful day. It had been wrong of Craig to leave Amy in the care of her sister, but even so Bethany blamed herself. Her grief was manifesting itself in seething anger which seemed to spill out of Bethany at every opportunity. She had taken to slamming her door and back-chatting her parents. Jessica was at a loss as to what to do. If she could, she would take her daughter to see a therapist, but Bethany emphatically refused to go. Perhaps once she had worked through some of her emotions, she would be more open to the idea. *If only she would talk to me*, Jessica thought to herself. It worried her terribly that Bethany was carrying the weight of the tragedy on her own. The poor girl must be tormented out of her mind. Jessica wished she could put her faith in God once again. Maybe then she would find rest and peace during the turmoil. But every time she considered turning towards him, red hot anger would writhe within her.

In the past, she had known God's love and experienced a close relationship with him.

After she had given birth to Bethany, Jessica hoped that in a couple of years she would be able to conceive again. But several years passed and still there was no sign or hope of her having another child. Eventually, she turned to God in desperation and began to pray for the second child she desperately wanted. Then, during one church service a woman prophesied that she would give birth to a female child.

Jessica held onto those words and nursed them in her heart until the day came when a blood test confirmed her pregnancy. She was ecstatic and so grateful to God for proving that his promises could be trusted. But now she was left feeling bereft and betrayed. Why would her heavenly Father grant her the desire of her heart only to take Amy away from her four years into her short life? Perhaps she had loved her child a little too much. Had she focused all her attention on her baby and turned away from the God she had served and worshiped? Even if that were the case, surely God would not spite her by taking Amy. Even in her ravaged and torn soul she knew that he was merciful and loving. There were no answers to her many questions. She would have to spend the rest of her life wrestling with her thoughts and trying to make sense of the tragedy that had fallen upon her.

Maybe she should join a support group. Perhaps it would help if she could talk to other mothers who had lost a child. She remembered her friend Beverly telling her about a group she had heard about. It was evident she needed help as she was drifting further and further away from Craig and their marriage was beginning to show cracks. They no longer shared the same bed and hardly spoke to each other. She was aware Craig was experiencing torment of his own. It was tragic that he blamed himself and Jessica knew she should be reaching out to him to help him overcome his pain. But she felt so consumed and overwhelmed by her own hurt that she had no energy or inclination to try.

There were many caring friends who had rallied around her during the first few weeks following Amy's death. But recently, the calls and visits had begun to dwindle until eventually Beverly was the only one who continued to show care and compassion towards her. Although she had never experienced the loss of a child, her friend had a nine-year old daughter who was recently diagnosed with sudden onset Type I diabetes. Every day she was faced with watching her child suffer as she injected insulin five times a day. It was a burden that she carried with the help of her faith in God. Through the tragedy, she had learnt to extend compassion to other hurting mothers and her continued support towards Jessica was of tremendous comfort to her.

Jessica decided to contact Beverly and chat to her about how she was feeling. Maybe she would have some advice for her. It was likely that she would talk about God and how he had been her comforter through her own ordeal, but maybe that was not a bad thing. At some point in time Jessica would have to invite God back into her heart. She would allow Beverly to talk about him, but at this stage she was not ready to turn back to him. Rising from the bed she turned and scanned Amy's bedroom. She picked up Amy's much-loved soft toy. It was a white kitten with a pink bow around its neck. 'Snowy' was so well loved, she was threadbare in places and the cotton around her little pink nose had begun to fray. Jessica stroked the toy almost as if it were a real cat. Somehow, she derived comfort from the feeling of its soft fur.

Jessica walked out of the bedroom holding the toy kitten. Walking into her bedroom she propped it against her pillows and smiled sadly.

She left her bedroom and closed the door behind her. Feeling ambushed by grief she made her way down the stairs and then rummaged in her handbag until she felt the smooth outline of her cell phone. Folding herself into the nearest chair, she closed her eyes and waited for Beverly to answer her call.

'Hi Jess, how are you doing?' Beverly said brightly.

'To be honest, I am not doing so well today. How are you? You sound out of breath.'

'Yes, I have just come in from a run around the common. Are you okay, Jess? Would you like me to come over?'

'No, don't worry...I'll be fine. The reason I am phoning is because I was wondering if you still have the flyer about that support group you were telling me about. Bev, I am really struggling to come to terms with Amy's death and I think I need help.'

'Oh Jess, of course I still have the flyer. In fact, I went to my first meeting on Thursday night. There were so many hurting women there. Two of the ladies have lost children. One of them lost her teenage son through suicide and the other lost her little boy through leukaemia. He was only five years old so I am sure you would really relate to her. It really is heart breaking to hear about all the tragedy these women have suffered. But it is not just a grief share group. It is open to all women who are suffering emotionally. I also met a lady who is in an abusive marriage. I think it is incredibly brave of her to attend the meetings. There is an honesty and vulnerability amongst the women that is very inspiring and comforting.'

'That sounds wonderful, Bev. I am so glad you have been to a meeting. I would not have the courage to go alone. When is the next one taking place?'

'The next meeting takes place on the first Thursday of next month. I would love you to join me and I can introduce you to Cindy. She is the lady who lost her little boy.'

'When did he die? Did she recently lose her child?'

'She said it happened eighteen months ago.' Bev answered softly.

'Oh... that's interesting. Did she mention that the pain gets better with time?'

'No, she said time has helped her to come to terms with her loss, but she shared how much it irritates her when people say that time heals. It is obvious that she is still experiencing a lot of pain. She is so honest and genuine. I think you will like her, Jess.'

'I will definitely attend the next meeting. Life feels so meaningless and bland now. I just don't know how I am going to get through this.'

'I can only imagine how hard it must be for you, my friend.' Beverley answered with concern. 'Is there anything I can do for you? You know I will come to visit you in a heartbeat.'

'Yes, Bev...I do know that. Thanks so much for your support but I will be fine. Besides, I must get dinner on the go in a minute. I am just going to have a hot bath and relax before I start cooking.'

'By the way, how is Craig doing? You don't talk about him much these days.'

'To be honest, I am not totally sure. It is clear he is still beating himself up for what happened, but he does not talk to me anymore. That is why I feel I need to start processing my pain so that I can reach out to him. I feel terrible that I am not being a very good wife. He has moved into the spare bedroom for now. It's as if he can't look me in the eye anymore.'

'I really wish there were something I could do. All I can say is I am here for you anytime you need me.'

'I really don't know what I would do without you, Bev. You have done so much for me already...'

'I feel like I haven't done enough.'

'You don't realise just how much you have helped...' Jessica's voice began to crack. 'I'm so sorry, Jess.' Beverley said with a sigh. 'Just remember I love you and I'm praying for you.'

'Thanks, I appreciate your prayers. I am finding it hard to pray these days.'

'God understands, sweetie.'

'I know, I keep telling myself he cares, but somehow my heart doesn't seem to register. I feel so alone and abandoned.'

'Well, I think that is natural under the circumstances. It is fine if you cannot pray. Just allow God to carry you through this dark night of the soul. He wants you to trust him in this.'

Jessica reached for a tissue and dabbed at her tear stained cheeks.

'At some stage I will be able to turn towards the Lord. But now I am still too angry. I cannot come to terms with why he would take my baby. It is just inconceivable that he could be so cruel. Anyway, enough of that.... I have been on the phone long enough and Craig won't be happy with another high phone bill.'

'I'll contact you again in a couple of days. When you feel up to it, you must all join us for dinner.' Beverley answered.

'That would be nice; I'll chat to you soon. Thanks for listening.'

'Bye, Jess. Take care of yourself.'

Jessica ended the call and put her cell phone down on the table next to her. The sense of desolation and loss overwhelmed her. She doubled over and began to weep into her hands.

***

Tiffany walked down the isle of the supermarket absent-mindedly throwing groceries into her shopping trolley. It had been a month since she had aborted her child and yet her every waking thought was consumed with images of the baby she had murdered. Jason had not spoken of their terrible act since it had happened. He seemed to have moved on without a backward glance.

Grief suddenly ambushed her as her eyes settled upon a pack of diapers. Aware that she was in a public place, she fought desperately hard to compose herself. Swallowing hard, she wiped her eyes and pushed her trolley past all the baby products which seemed to deliberately taunt her. The voices in her head were growing louder every day and nothing seemed to silence them. She had killed an innocent child and it was as simple as that. One day she would have to stand before God and give account for what she had done. She felt as if she was submerged in a tomb of guilt. No matter how hard she tried she could not escape it.

Her relationship with Jason was strained to breaking point. He had no tolerance for her tears and remorse. Perhaps he was dealing with his grief simply by denying the whole act altogether. It bothered Tiffany that he did not seem to want to talk to her about it. Hadn't they made the decision together? This burden was not hers to carry alone. If he truly loved her, surely, he would be more supportive? The nagging thought that he was pulling away from her pervaded her every minute of the day. She had decided to get rid of the child because she did not want to lose Jason. But what if he had plans to move on? Tiffany had no idea where she stood with him anymore.

The thought that perhaps he did not really love her hovered at the back of her mind like a stranger knocking on the door of her house. It was always there – the disturbing thought that maybe her whole relationship was a farce. It bothered her that somehow Jason seemed to have moved past the whole experience. Did he realise that

they had both killed their unborn child? He certainly never found the need to talk about it or express any kind of regret over his actions. Why should she be the one to carry the guilt on her shoulders? Yes, her body had been violated and she was responsible for murdering her child. But he was the one who had made the decision and then pressurised her into his way of thinking. Resentment grew within her. Love was being replaced by seething anger and disappointment. How would she be able to move past this and build a life with the man who had told her to kill her unborn child? But why was she finding it so hard to leave him?

On some level she still loved him and was hoping that she would be able to make atonement for her sins through having Jason's child one day. Even so, another baby would not replace the one she had lost. Part of her felt as if she knew him. A strange, instinctive feeling had overcome her when she first found out she was pregnant. She just knew her first child would be a son. Now, in the cold, harsh reality of what she had done she felt gutted and desperately alone in her grief. If only she had known this would happen. She wished she had taken the time to really, truly think it through. She felt so angry and betrayed on so many levels. The doctor at the clinic had told her it was only 'a mass of cells.' The truth that it was a life complete with a heartbeat had been almost ignored and overlooked. Tiffany felt hoodwinked and cheated. She had been robbed of a part of herself which she could never get back.

Although her child would never be born, she still felt like a mother grieving the loss of a person who would have meant the world to her. She would never see his first smile or hear him call her mama. Tiffany would never watch him playing in the park or feel the warm comfort of his grubby little hand in hers. There would be no birthday parties complete with jumping castles and puppet shows. Her child would never know just how deep and wide and all-consuming her love would be for him.

As she approached the cashier, Tiffany fumbled around in her handbag to avoid making eye contact. She reached into the trolley and methodically lined up her groceries. The cashier hurried through the task of adding them up. Tiffany paid with her credit card and then looked away. Her eyes glistened with tears and she was feeling extremely vulnerable and exposed. Almost as if everyone in the supermarket knew she had murdered her child. Every time she passed a mother with a child in her arms, she was convinced the infant was somehow judging her. Clutching her bag of groceries to her chest, she rushed out of the busy supermarket and into the bleak winter's day. She shivered as the cold wind nipped at her fingers. The grey sky streaked with impending rain clouds only mirrored the distress which rumbled like thunder across her tortured soul.

Tiffany hurried to catch the number fifty-nine bus which would take her almost to her doorstep in Ealing Broadway. Once aboard the bus she sank into the first empty seat and breathed a sigh of relief. She wondered if she were becoming agoraphobic as every venture outside of her house was becoming more difficult. It took all her resolve just to climb out of bed every morning and battle the rush hour commuters to get into work. At least at work she could immerse herself in her tasks and find some sense of solace. At work there were no reminders of babies to taunt her. It somehow seemed to be the only safe place. At home there were constantly occasions where friends popped in with their children.

It was also becoming increasingly difficult to find feasible excuses as to why she did not want to attend yet another baby shower, christening or children's birthday party. Only Tiffany's select few best friends knew what lurked behind her feeble excuses. Most of the couple's friends and acquaintances had no idea what she was dealing with. They just assumed that the once bubbly, outgoing and fun-loving girl with the bright, open smile and sunny disposition was a little under the weather.

Tiffany stared aimlessly out the window and found herself wondering about the lives of the people walking by. Had any of the women had abortions? Were any of them pregnant and contemplating such an act? Maybe some of them had already had abortions. She wondered if she would forever feel like a giant baby size hole was carved into her heart. Would she always feel incomplete and utterly bereft and broken into a million pieces? On some level she fervently believed that one day when she had a child of her own the pain would begin to recede from her life.

Jason's only comment about the subject had been exactly that.

'Tiff, we will have a baby one day, and everything will be fine.' How could he possibly believe that another child would simply replace the one they had lost? It was inconceivable that he thought it was a simple trade. It was clear he really had no idea how she was feeling and in fact, that comment had just made her feel that he was diminishing the magnitude of her loss. Resentment seethed within her. Most often she could contain her anger and bitterness towards Jason but when he had made that frivolous and insensitive comment, in that moment she had wanted to bash him over the head with a shovel.

***

As Charlotte skimmed through the back page of the daily newspaper her interest was piqued by the advertisement in the bottom corner. *Apples of Gold Women's Support Group.* The bold letters seemed to scream out to her. *Are you struggling with a wound from your past, or do you feel like life has thrown one too many curve balls at you? Then this group is for you. Meetings take place at Pitshanger Community Hall, first Thursday of every month.*

She leaned back in her chair and contemplated the contents of the advert. Charlotte could not deny that she was going through life pretending she was happy when the truth was that she embroiled in her worst nightmare. She felt like one of those swans she had recently seen down by the river...so serene, gliding through the water whilst under the surface its legs were feverishly paddling back and forth to give it momentum. Even Charlotte's church group were not aware of her struggles. It was time for her to get help and this *Apples of Gold* group sounded ideal.

Charlotte berated herself once again for leaving late. As she walked into the Community Hall a dozen heads swiveled like a bunch of meerkats to see what the intrusion was. There was a handful of women sitting on chairs arranged in a circle all blinking against the harsh fluorescent lighting which flickered occasionally. The air was marinated with the smell of stale beer most likely left over from a party in the hall the day before.

'Sorry, I'm late.' A hesitant smile tugged at the corner of her mouth as she sat down on the only available seat. Charlotte caught the eye of the woman sitting next to her. She was mixed race and very striking with long braided hair and she appeared to be very uncomfortable.

The meeting consisted of woman of various ages. As the facilitator welcomed the newcomers Diane surreptitiously glanced around the room. This was the first support group of any kind she had ever attended, and she was finding the experience very stressful. Even so, she knew it was where she needed to be if she hoped to ever be free of the demons relentlessly hounding her.

During the meeting, Susan Banks the group's facilitator turned to her audience and asked 'would any of you like to share anything? This is a safe forum, so there is nothing to be afraid of. We are all here because we are struggling with a hurt that is crippling our lives. Apples of Gold are here to help you find your way back to healing and wholeness. There is no judgement here.'

A dry breath escaped just before Diane dissolved into tears. As hard as she tried, she could not seem to compose herself. The room grew strangely quiet as she continued to sob. Like a soft feather, she felt the brush of a tissue against her knee. Looking up, she was moved by the compassion and warmth in the liquid brown eyes of the young girl sitting next to her.

'Thank you,' Diane said taking the tissue. She noticed that the girl's face was streaked with tears and wondered why. How could a girl so young carry such a depth of tragedy and heart break?

Diane dabbed at her face to mop up her tears and then squared her shoulders.

'I would like to share,' she said. Her voice was strangled with tears.

'I was sexually abused as a young child. For some many years I buried the pain and I thought I was coping. But recently, since I turned forty a few weeks ago, I've begun to unravel.'

Diane lifted her eyes from her lap and looked around the room. Some of the women were nodding and others had tears in their eyes. For a few brief seconds, Diane allowed herself to be cocooned in the warmth and solidarity she felt in the group.

'Diane, it is very brave of you to speak out about the abuse. You have made the first step, so well done. During our meetings we will examine your feelings and help you to find the peace that you crave. You will find healing here. It's a safe place,' said Susan.

'Would anyone else like to share?'

Diane locked eyes with a beautiful redhead. Her pale face was devoid of make-up and her long hair was loosely tied up in a messy bun on the top of her head. There was a dusting of freckles across her nose which added to her charm. Diane instantly liked her.

Jessica raised her hand.

'I'd like to share,' she said. Her voice cracked as tears pooled in her eyes. 'A few weeks ago, I lost my daughter, Amy. She was just four years old and she drowned in my swimming pool. My husband was supposed to be watching her…'

'Jessica, I'm so deeply sorry for your loss. Do you blame yourself for your daughter's death?' Asked Susan.

Jessica nodded. Her voice was barely a whisper. 'Yes, I do. I had popped out to do some grocery shopping when it happened. I should have been there. I failed my baby.'

Several of the women in the group shook their heads.

'It's not your fault, Jessica. This group will help you to see that and forgive yourself.'

Susan's voice was warm and soothing. Would anyone else like to share about why you have come to this group?'

Tiffany raised her hand. Her eyes darted around the room. Was she really in a safe place? Would these women understand, or would they judge her? She was willing to take a chance.

'I um...' Tiffany choked on the words she knew she had to get out. 'I had an abortion last week. My boyfriend insisted that I get rid of the baby. It was either go through the procedure or risk losing him. But I regret it so much and am consumed with guilt over it.'

Tiffany looked down at her hands folded in her lap and tried to blink back the tears. Eventually, like a wave crashing on the shore, she allowed her emotions to wash over her and watched her tears drip onto her fingers.

'I'm so sorry Tiffany, I can see you are in a great deal of pain. It is very traumatic to go through an abortion. But I can assure you that as you unpack your feelings and get to grips with your loss, you will find closure. You will even be able to forgive yourself,' Susan said.

We will break for tea in a few minutes but before we do, does anyone else want to share?'

Charlotte nodded.

'Yes, I do,' she said.

'I am a victim of domestic abuse. My husband is a heavy drinker and a complicated man. Whenever he drinks too much...which is often, he beats me.'

Charlotte pulled up the sleeves of her jersey to reveal angry purple bruises on both her wrists. A few of the women gasped.

'I know I need to leave him, but I am scared about what he will do. I've left him a few times in the past and he always finds me and threatens me with all sorts of unspeakable things.' Tears trembled in her wide, imploring eyes which were road-mapped with tiny red veins. Her slim, birdlike body trembled under the gaze of every women in the room.

Diane leaned forward and tugged at the tissues in the box on the table. She stood up and handed one to Charlotte.

'Thank you,' the women's eyes met and for a second Charlotte felt as if she was being seen. Truly seen. The compassion and understanding in Diane's eyes drew her to the tall, blond woman standing before her. Even though she had only just met her for the first time, in that one small gesture Charlotte felt they had made a deep soul connection.

The atmosphere in the room changed dramatically once the meeting was over and refreshments served. Although all who were there knew it was necessary to attend, a collective sigh of relief was breathed. The rattle of teacups and scent of freshly baked cake drew the women to the back of the hall.

Diane decided to go outside to smoke a cigarette. Her hands shook as she lit it and inhaled deeply. She heard the door open and Abigail stepped outside. She was a curvaceous woman with jet black shoulder length hair, olive skin and doe shaped brown eyes. Diane assumed that she must be Spanish or Brazilian. Abigail's face lit up when she saw Diane.

'Oh good, another smoker. I was worried I was the only one.'

Diane smiled.

'Nope, you are not alone. I've been craving a cigarette ever since the meeting started!'

Abigail giggled. 'Me too,' she said.

Diane read the name tag the woman was wearing. Curious about why she was at the meeting, she decided to go ahead and ask.

'So, Abigail, you've heard my story. What brings you to the support group?

'Well, to be honest, I feel a bit silly being here. My story is not as tragic as some others. I found out a couple of weeks ago that my husband is having an affair.'

'Oh dear, I'm sorry to hear that.' Said Diane.

'But don't diminish your pain. You may not have been abused or gone through an abortion, but a spouse cheating is still heart breaking.'

Abigail nodded. 'Thanks for understanding.'

The door opened and Jessica, Tiffany and Charlotte stepped outside. They had been chatting to each other over tea and cake and were desperate for a breath of fresh air.

'Charlotte,' said Diane. 'I think it was very brave of you to come to the support group.

Does your husband know you are here?'

Charlotte shook her head.

'No, I told him I was going to visit a friend. He would be incensed if he knew I had joined a support group. He already thinks I'm weak and pathetic.'

'Oh, that old chestnut,' said Abigail.

'The abuser will always tear down your self-esteem like that. I know as before I married my husband, I was involved in an abusive relationship when I was still living in Brazil. He is the reason I left my homeland and moved to the UK. My father is British and living here. He helped me to escape. Charlotte, I know you may feel that you'll never be free but it's not true.'

Charlotte nodded.

'Yes, I know that one day I will escape from his clutches. I just have to come up with a plan and find the courage to follow it.'

Diane felt protective of the younger woman.

'We'll help you,' she said with a reassuring edge to her voice.

'I have an idea. Let us all pop over to the nearest pub for a drink so we can get to know each other better.' Diane said.

'Yes, I would love that,' said Charlotte.

'You can count me in,' said Abigail.

'I could come for a quick drink as my husband is looking after my daughter,' said Jessica.

'I need a drink after coming clean about the abortion. It is the first time I have opened up about it to anybody. It is both cathartic and frightening at the same time,' said Tiffany.

'Great, let us get our coats and head over to the Slug and Lettuce over the road,' said Diane.

The cold, February wind nipped at their heels as they crossed the street. The pub seemed to throw open its arms and welcome them inside like an old friend.

Diane took the lead in ordering drinks at the bar and the rest of the women found a table in a corner next to a roaring fire.

As the women chatted, they found comfort and solidarity in their mutual pain. They all realised that strong friendships were being formed. As they all felt safe and heard, their individual personalities emerged. Diane was the quietest woman in the group. As she was an introverted, analytical person she preferred to just sit and listen. Charlotte was as colourful as the floral dress that she wore, and her beautiful almond shaped green eyes lit up when she spoke about her painting.

'I would love to see your art, Charlotte.' Said Diane.

'You can come over sometime when my husband is not at home. I will let you know. Let me take your phone number, Diane.'

'Let us all exchange phone numbers,' said Tiffany. Her voice was soft and honey smooth. She had a beautiful complexion and her large brown eyes held so much emotion and naked honesty.

'I write poetry,' said Tiffany. 'At the moment, I am negotiating a deal with a publisher. I am so excited. I have written a few poems about the abortion. My writing helps me so much. If it were not for my poetry, I don't think I would be able to get out of bed in the morning.'

'What do you do for a living, Tiffany?' Asked Jessica.

'I have my own florist. It was my dream for the longest time and then finally last year, I secured a loan and was able to open my own shop. I love working with flowers and it keeps me out of mischief. What do you do?'

'I have my own company in interior design,' replied Jessica. 'I've been going for over ten years now.'

'Oh, how wonderful,' said Abigail.

'Thanks, what line of work are you in?'

'I am a graphic designer, but I gave up my career when I had my children so now, I am a stay at home mum. When my children are older, I'd like to start my own company and work from home.'

'I love your accent, Abigail. And, you are simply beautiful. You look like a model,' said Tiffany. 'Where are you from originally?'

'Oh, you are so kind, Tiffany. I am from Brazil, but I moved to the UK when I married Richard. He is British and I met him when he was on holiday in Brazil.

'But that's enough about me,' said Abigail. 'Diane, what do you do for a living?'

Diane smiled and put down her gin and tonic. Finally, a topic she felt comfortable with.

'I'm a lawyer,' she said.

'I specialise in criminal law.'

'Wow, that must be very interesting,' said Tiffany.

'Yes, it is. It keeps me busy. I work very long hours which is exhausting but I'm passionate about my work.'

The women finished their drinks and bid farewell to each other with promises to meet again outside the Apples of Gold support group. Over the following weeks, the bonds of friendship grew strong between them. They spoke to each other almost every day.

With Charlotte's fortieth birthday just around the corner, Diane had suggested they surprise her by meeting at her house armed with champagne and sushi. They all arrived within minutes of each other.

'Girls, she doesn't know we are coming so you need to be quiet now,' Diane said raising her forefinger to her lips. The friends quietened down and walked up the garden path. But just as Jessica was about to ring the doorbell, a crash was heard inside the house followed by a high-pitched scream. The girls exchanged concerned glances and lunged for the door. Opening it they charged into the house.

'Who the hell do you think you are?' Patrick bellowed. His face was flushed red with anger and the veins in his neck protruded and convulsed like earthworms under his skin. The air was cloaked with stale alcohol. The girls converged in the kitchen. Patrick had Charlotte pinned against the wall with his large hands gripped tightly around her throat. She was lifted clear off the ground and her wide, frightened eyes begged for mercy. Tears of shame and humiliation coursed down her cheeks and dampened her floral blouse. It was blood soaked. Pockets of dark bruises had started to converge around her eyes.

Diane was the first of the group to call out. 'Stop it! You are going to kill her!' For a second, Patrick turned away from Charlotte and addressed the ladies with venom saturating his voice. 'Get the hell out of my house! This is none of your business.'

Jessica was overcome with rage at the sight of her friend's blatant abuse at the hands of her husband. She lunged towards him and tried to loosen his grip on Charlotte's throat. Patrick lashed out violently and threw Jessica against the wall. 'Get off me' he yelled. He put his full weight into hurling the petite woman away from him. She was knocked unconscious by the force of the blow and slumped like a broken ragdoll in the corner of the room. Tiffany raced to her side.

All the girls began to shout at once.

'Stop it!' They screamed.

Somehow, their plea to leave their friend alone seemed to spur him on. Patrick tightened his grip around his wife's throat. Charlotte's face began to turn blue. Her glassy, bloodshot eyes mirrored an emptiness which indicated she had given up the fight. Patrick was a large, heavyset man and none of the girls in the room were a match for him. Diane knew something drastic needed to be done to save Charlotte.

Diane glimpsed Tiffany cradling Jessica's head in her lap. She was attempting to stop the blood flow from a gash in her forehead. In that moment, Diane was consumed by a rage which ignited within her. Immediately, she burned with superhuman strength.

'You bastard!' She grabbed the skillet on the kitchen counter and swung it at his head. He hit the floor with a loud thud and for a few seconds the room was strangely quiet. Diane dropped the skillet and hunched over herself as the bile rose into her throat. She grabbed a bucket sitting under the sink and vomited into it with all the violence with which she had attacked Patrick.

Once she was certain her stomach had been purged of its contents, Diane wiped her mouth and straightened up. The reality that she could have killed him began to settle upon her like a thick ominous fog. The adrenaline rush she had experienced gave way to bone numbing exhaustion. Her knees buckled beneath her and she slipped to the floor. She crawled over to where Charlotte was curled in the corner weeping.

'Charlie, you are safe now.' She whispered. The terrified woman nodded her head slowly and turned to face her friend. 'What happened? I remember Patrick trying to throttle me, but everything is a blank after that.' Purple stains from the imprints of her husband's fingers had marked the delicate pale skin of her throat. Charlotte kicked Patrick's foot in irritation. As her kick shifted his body a dark, sticky pool of blood began to spread around him.

Diane was alerted to the sound of moaning coming from the corner of the kitchen. She looked up. Tiffany padded softly towards her with her arm around Jessica who grimaced in pain.

Charlotte's voice pierced Diane's thoughts. 'Is he dead?' She asked through dry, cracked lips. Her friends exchanged frightened glances. 'I don't know,' Diane said. 'I had to do something Charlie. He was going to kill you. In fact, he almost did.'

'Yes, I know,' Charlotte replied. He lost his temper because I was late getting home and had not cooked his dinner. I knew this day would come. But I thought I would be the one to do the deed, not you.' She crouched over his body and felt his neck for a pulse. It was very weak. 'He will die of loss of blood if we don't call an ambulance soon,' Charlotte said. Her eyes were wide and beseeching, almost as if she were begging for absolution. Diane grabbed her by the hand and pulled her to her feet.

'You have to think clearly now, Charlie. This could be your ticket out of your abusive marriage. How many times have you told me he is a cruel narcissist who torments you continually? As far as I am concerned, he can rot in hell!'

Charlotte nodded. Everything her friend was saying made perfect sense to her. She put down the phone she had gripped in her hand. She knew she had to do the right thing and call 999 but the thought of simply not making that call was very enticing.

'I have to call the paramedics, Di. Much as I despise the man, I cannot let him die here like this. There must be another way out of this hellish marriage of mine.'

Charlotte reached into her pocket and took out a packet of cigarettes. She lit it hastily and inhaled. She turned to look at Diane.

'Di, please can you make the call. I just don't feel up to it.' Diane nodded.

'Yes, hello,' she said. 'We have a man with a head wound and he's bleeding profusely. Please come quickly. OK, hold on.'

Diane passed the cell phone to Charlotte.

'They need your address,' she said.

'Hello, I live at number five Foxglove Gardens, Ealing Broadway SW6 9TJ. OK, thank you.'

Suddenly a shadow passed across the glass of the front door followed by the sound of the doorbell. Diane looked from one woman to the next and lifted her forefinger to her lips. "Sssh," she said and gestured for them to all get down so that they would not be seen. For a few tension-filled moments the room was completely quiet except for the tick-tock of the grandfather clock in the hallway. Whoever was at the front door grew impatient and rang the doorbell a second time. Jessica looked around the room.

'Maybe if we just wait here and keep quiet, they will go away,' she whispered. The rest of the women all nodded at once.

'Charlie, are you home?' A woman's voice called from outside. 'Hello, anyone home? Diane stood up slowly. 'It's Abigail,' she said. 'What do we do now? Maybe we should we let her in and tell her what happened.' Tiffany said.

'I just need to think for a minute,' Diane answered. 'I don't want to implicate her in what happened tonight. Let us wait a couple of minutes. If she refuses to leave, then we will let her in.'

The women waited for Abigail to leave. After ringing the doorbell, a couple more times she eventually turned and walked away.

The emergency crew arrived within fifteen minutes and strapped Patrick to a stretcher.

'I think we arrived here just in time, Mam.' Said Simon, the paramedic. Charlotte simply nodded.

***

Diane was looking forward to getting home and unwinding with a glass of wine. Everything about the day felt surreal. She could not get her head around the fact that she had almost killed a man. The sound he made as he hit the floor would be forever etched into her mind. Whenever the guilt began to snake its way through her, she would remind herself that her friend had almost lost her life that night. The look of terror in Charlotte's eyes and the blue tinge to her skin would always haunt her. At the time, Diane was the only one in the room who had the courage to act. She would always tell herself that it had been the right course of action. Patrick's vice-like grip on Charlotte's throat had threatened to drain the life out of her. If Diane had not intervened at that exact moment, Charlie would not have survived.

Diane pulled into her driveway with a sigh. She was bone achingly tired and she felt as if she had already lived through a dozen lifetimes. As she unlocked her front door, she found herself thinking that certain things in her life needed to change. For a start, she needed to stop seeing David. How had she turned into an adulteress and a murderer as well? She had certainly fallen so far from grace. No longer was she the innocent young girl who had led the local church's youth group so many years ago.

Casually dropping her handbag on the table in the hall, she walked into the kitchen and opened the pantry. She was relieved to find that the bottle of Cabernet was still there. She poured herself a glass and walked through to her lounge. Sinking gratefully into the chair nearest the fireplace, she closed her eyes and savored her first sip of wine. Her husband had sent a message to inform her that he would be meeting clients for drinks after work. Diane was relishing the solitude and instead of missing him, she was hoping he would say away for a few more heavenly hours. It was not that she did not love him. It was simply that being with him only intensified her guilt over her affair. Spending time alone with her thoughts was exactly what she needed right now. There was no one around to muddy the water or bring further confusion into her already complicated life.

Diane's thoughts were interrupted by the shrill sound of her mobile phone ringing. She stood up reluctantly and padded through to her dining room. Rustling through her handbag she struggled to locate her phone. In sheer frustration she tipped it upside down until it regurgitated its contents and surrendered her phone.

'Hello.' Diane said with a weary edge to her voice.

'Di, hi it's me,' Charlotte said.

'Hi Charlie, what's up?'

'Patrick has just been admitted to the operating theatre. There's bleeding on his brain and he is in a coma. The doctor's not sure if he'll ever wake up from it.'

'How do you feel about that, Charlie?'

'I just feel numb. It all feels very weird, as if it's happening to somebody else.'

'I can imagine. Just remember I am here for you my friend.'

'Thanks, Di. I appreciate that.'

'Do you want me to pop over and visit you? I don't like the thought of you being alone right now.'

'No, thanks. Really, I am fine. I'm just going to have a bath and then go to bed.

'Bye, Charlie. Take care and stay strong.'

Diane put her mobile phone down on the coffee table and walked through to the kitchen to replenish her glass. She thought better of it and instead carried the bottle through to the lounge. The combination of the roaring fire and the wine was beginning to warm her. It felt good to finally relax. She poured herself into her chair and put her feet up on the table. The chair seemed to embrace her aching body.

It was at times such as this that she longed to close her eyes and fall asleep. But she knew that she would not find solace and refuge in her slumber. Instead, the demons would crawl out of the shadows and torment her with memories of the sexual abuse. And, the memories would birth intense feelings of rage and fear. She wondered if perhaps she was still waiting for someone to come along and save that six-year old child. It occurred to her that perhaps that was why she was the first to jump in and save her friend. She knew exactly how it felt to be vulnerable and powerless.

***

Charlotte locked her front door and began to walk briskly up the High Street. It was a cold, frosty morning so she pulled on her gloves. Ambivalence over her husband' demise was something she wrestled with every moment of the day since Diane had hit Patrick with the skillet. There was no love lost in the marriage as it had been wrung out and obliterated by years of cruelty from the man she had promised to 'honour and obey.' Now, all she felt for the man was distain. She desperately wanted to be free of his clutches but if he died would Diane be convicted of manslaughter?

She found herself thinking back to all the many times he had beaten her. She should have known that he was a narcissistic misogynist. But when she had first met him there had been no tell-tale signs. He was a young medical student studying to become a surgeon and she was a waitress at the local deli. She had no idea that her life would spiral out of control once she had married him. Patrick had been so different back then. The first time she set eyes on him she had fallen for his boyish charm and wide, alluring smile. He was so confident and full of life. She was a shy seventeen-year-old who knew nothing about the world, and most especially the ways of men.

Having grown up in Cornwall, she had lived a relatively sheltered life. When she decided to move to London, she had no idea that she would meet her future husband there. But the first time Patrick walked into the deli she knew there was something different about him. When she handed over his steaming cup of coffee with extra cinnamon, their hands had briefly touched and a spark had been ignited. As her face turned red under his penetrating gaze, she knew in that instant that he would be back. And he was…the next day and the day after that. Each morning he waited patiently in the queue until he was served by her. If one of the other girls offered to serve him, he refused and said he was waiting to speak to Charlotte. As a result, the girls teased her mercilessly.

'When is Don Juan coming in?' They would ask. Every day, he had eyes only for her. Eventually, one morning he leaned towards her as she passed him the coffee and whispered in her ear… 'What is your phone number, Charlie?' She laughed and carried on serving the customers as if nothing had happened. The following day Patrick did not come in. Charlotte found herself missing him and hoping that he would come back. A few days passed and still he did not come into the deli. Charlotte began to wonder if perhaps he had moved away. But then finally he did come in again. This time she was ready for him and just before she handed Patrick his usual order, she scribbled her phone number on the side of his coffee cup.

Thinking about those days brought the realisation that even back then he was playing with her emotions. He had master-minded the game and deliberately stayed away from the coffee shop for a few days to reel her in like an unsuspecting fish lured by bait on a hook. Charlotte had been so naive and innocent that she just thought it was romantic. Now, she just felt like a fool for not seeing the truth about him.

A whirlwind romance ensued after that. Patrick was adept at making sure that each date was more impressive and exciting than the one before. He surprised her with tickets to the stage show 'Phantom of the Opera' and always arrived to fetch her armed with a bunch of her favourite lilies. On one occasion he bought her an elegant wristwatch just because he could. He proceeded to bombard her with expensive gifts and tickets to exotic locations. They travelled the world together. Their first holiday together was a week on a yacht in Turkey. They visited the markets together where he bought her a beautiful, handmade Kilim rug. They had enjoyed their time in Turkey together so much, that they had recently celebrated their ten-year anniversary there. On that occasion, Patrick had bought her a Persian carpet to commemorate their anniversary.

Charlotte and Patrick had dated for six months before they decided to move in together. She had left her cramped bedsit in Battersea Park and taken up residence in swanky Notting Hill. Her doting boyfriend seemed to hang on her every word and for a while life seemed to be everything she had ever dreamed of. Even when he lost his temper and belittled her over something inconsequential, she overlooked his short comings. Any cruelty from his side was always swiftly followed by apologies accompanied by beautiful bouquets of flowers, or bottles of perfume. Charlotte soon learnt to cope with the emotional and psychological fallout of his bullying. She convinced herself that there were so many positive characteristics about Patrick that this seemingly small problem could be overlooked. Little did she know that his narcissistic ways would soon trap her in a tomb of fear and torment.

Her thoughts began to wander back to some of the worst experiences she had known during the years she was with Patrick. On one occasion whilst on their way back from a party they had disagreed about something small. They were waiting on the platform at the Covent Garden underground station. Patrick had drunk too much and was argumentative and belligerent. He grabbed Charlotte by the lapels of her jacket and shoved her towards the edge of the platform. Although she fought him, Patrick was too strong for her and easily overpowered her delicate frame. Eventually, he pushed until she was leaning over the platform and in the path of the oncoming train. Charlotte remembered looking into his black eyes and feeling as if she was staring into the pits of hell.

'Don't argue with me,' he sneered. 'I am always right.'

He then whisked her away from the edge of the platform and shoved her against the inside wall. By that stage Charlotte was shaking like a leaf. Terrified tears full of shame and humiliation coursed down her cheeks. In that moment, she vowed she would leave him as soon as she returned to their apartment. But, by the time she arrived home she was exhausted and soon fell into a deep, dreamless sleep.

The next morning Patrick surprised her with breakfast in bed. He walked into their bedroom grinning like a Cheshire cat. He was carrying a tray laden with fruit, pastries and freshly squeezed orange juice. No mention was made of the night before. Charlotte was so bowled over by his surprising behaviour that she was afraid to mention what had transpired between them. He placed the tray on the bed and then sat down next to her. Caressing her face, he looked deeply into her eyes.

Her heart stopped as she remembered staring into those same black eyes the night before. How was it possible that they could look so different in the cold harsh light of day? All the suppressed feelings of sheer terror came rushing back and her eyes filled with tears. But once again, Patrick took control of the situation. He wiped the tears from her face and leant towards her until his lips caressed hers.

'I love you Charlie. You are the most beautiful woman in the world.' In that instant, all was forgotten. She was sucked into his devious world where she was his puppet and he was her master.

Charlie tried to shrug the memory from her mind and quickened her pace. She needed to reach the bank before it closed. As she entered Wimbledon High Street a feeling of peace settled over her. Seeing the crowds mulling around the shops brought a sense of familiarity and she reminded herself that today was a new day. Patrick was gone from her life for now and she wasn't sure if he was going to survive the head wound. The neurological surgeon had said that the next twenty-four hours were crucial. All she could do now was wait.

***

It had been six weeks since Jessica lost her precious little girl. But still it felt as if there was a massive, gaping chasm in her heart. Every breath seemed to hurt and no matter how many times she told herself to try and move on, she just could not seem to do it.

Craig and Bethany were both dealing with their grief in their own individual ways. Craig had thrown himself into his work and seemed to spend more time away from home than with his family. Jessica was certain he was avoiding her. He blamed himself for the death of his daughter and much as Jessica tried to convince herself that it was not his fault, in her heart she felt angry with him. Every time she looked into his eyes, she saw unbelievable guilt and pain mirrored there. So, it became easier to just not look at him.

On that fateful day when she left Amy in Craig's care, it never occurred to her that he would not take his responsibility seriously. He was otherwise an excellent father and always had been. When Jessica lost her first husband to cancer five years ago, she had thought it would not be possible to love again. But when she met Craig through mutual friends, love had indeed bloomed, and their bond was a happy one. There had been no marital problems to speak of. Not until that fateful day.

Jessica's heart broke every time she thought of her teenage daughter. She knew that she was carrying a huge amount of guilt and blamed herself for her little sister's death. It enraged Jessica that Craig had been so irresponsible in passing off his duty onto Bethany. It was excruciatingly painful that not only had they lost Amy, but the entire family was falling apart as a result. Instead of finding comfort in each other, each family member was burying their grief.

Jessica decided it was time they went for family counselling. Her marriage would not survive unless they did something soon. Craig had not touched her in months and when he did come home from the office, he usually reeked of alcohol. This was particularly alarming to Jessica as her husband had hardly ever touched a drink. Now it seemed he was drowning his sorrows almost every day.

Jessica was really pleased that she had followed her instincts and joined the Apples of Gold Support Group. She had toyed with the idea for weeks before deciding to go. The first time she had arrived there, she had felt so conspicuous and awkward. Her raw, naked pain was evident to all who met her. But she later discovered that every one of the women there had felt the same way. As she got to know them, she saw that although their stories and tragedies were different, the pain and feelings of powerlessness they shared were the same.

When Tiffany had shared about the abortion she had been coerced into, her heart had melted. It gave her a glimpse into the true power of a mother's love. Even though Tiffany had never held her child in her arms she still loved her baby. Why else would she be suffering the way she was? Jessica realised that there was a bonding in their mutual loss.

***

Jessica finished off the last of the ironing and then packed it away into the various closets. She walked down the hallway and then stopped at the door to Amy's room. She had not been able to pack it up or get rid of any of her things. For now, she wanted it left exactly as her daughter had left it. A single tear inched down her cheek.

She checked her watch. In a few minutes Craig would be home and then they were due to visit her therapist. This would be their third session. The first two had been disastrous. When Carol, the counsellor had asked each of them how they felt about the tragedy, all the gruesome details and innermost feelings had been unmasked. Jessica felt ashamed of her feelings of anger and blame towards Craig as she knew he was in a lot of pain over the tragedy. The truth was that she did not want to feel that way towards her husband. She wanted to be able to help him through his grief and set him free from his guilt. But no matter how hard she tried she could not seem to reach him without letting slip how angry she was deep down inside. Jessica loved him deeply but lately had begun to wonder if love alone was enough to sustain their marriage. Since losing Amy their otherwise happy union had taken on a new nature. It had become dark, lonely and cold and Jessica felt as if she was dying inside the tomb of grief and shattered dreams.

She was pulled from her thoughts by the sound of a car door slamming. A few minutes later she heard Craig open the front door and dump his briefcase down on the dining room table.

'Hi Jess.'

Jessica fixed a smile on her face and walked towards him.

'Hi sweetheart,' the words seemed to stick in her throat like shards of glass.

She kissed him lightly on the lips and then snaked her arms around his neck. Pulling him towards her she inhaled the musky aroma of his aftershave. She closed her eyes and allowed her body to relax against his for a few seconds.

'What time is our appointment?' Craig asked.

'We have to be there by six. Are you ready to go?'

Craig nodded. 'Yes, we had better get going then. Take your coat as its cold outside.'

They walked outside in silence and Jessica waited for Craig to open the car door for her. It warmed her that her husband still took the time to treat her like a lady. His manners had impressed her right from the first day she had met him.

The therapist's office was only a short drive away from Jessica and Craig's home. They arrived within a few minutes.

The receptionist looked up as they walked into the counsellor's office. She smiled and gestured for them to take a seat.

'Carol will be with you shortly.'

Jessica smiled. 'Thank you, Patricia.'

Carol opened the door of her office and escorted a young boy out. She looked up and spotted Jessica and Craig waiting for her.

'Please come through…' The couple got up and walked into the therapist's office. They sat down and waited for Carol to join them.

'Right,' said Carol. 'The last couple of weeks we have talked a lot about your marriage and why you are here. But today I want to delve into your daughter's death. It is very common for couples to separate and end up divorced after losing a child. A tragedy like this is enormously taxing on you each as individual parents and on your marriage. Very few marriages survive. But it is possible, and I am hoping that I will be able to work through the issues with you. If you can both be unlocked to grieve in a healthy way instead of bottling it up inside, then you have a fighting chance. Too often couples blame each other or just withdraw from one another as a coping mechanism. But I hope to teach you how to comfort and support each other.'

***

Charlotte left the bank and walked down the High Street. Her experience of her husband told her that should he live, she would be in for the punishment of her life. Patrick would blame her for what happened. It was most likely he would come after her and finish the job he had started that night.

As her thoughts raced, she quickened her pace. She needed to speak to Diane and ask her advice. Her friend was always so level-headed. Charlotte was certain she would know what to do. She considered packing a suitcase and leaving the house. It has been two days since she saw him.

Charlotte had not worked for a living in years. She was a housewife who was entirely dependent on her husband financially. But it had not always been that way. When she met Patrick, he had been studying medicine and she was working as a waitress in a deli. Secretly, she had always wanted to be a nurse, but her parents did not have the means to put her through university. So, she had shelved her dreams and got a job to help her father look after her sickly mother. But once her mother died, her cruel, alcoholic father chased her out of the house. It was then that she decided it was time to pursue her goals. So, she worked during the day and studied until the wee hours of the morning. It took her longer that she anticipated but eventually she graduated with honours.

She decided to specialise in midwifery. The years she spent at Queen Charlotte's Hospital in Hammersmith were the best of her life. She was a natural in everything and patients responded well to her warm and caring nature. There was a period of a few years when Patrick seemed to be doting on her and it was only after they were married that the dark side of his personality began to emerge. There were times when he seemed cold and distant and Charlotte found that she could not get close to him. He kept his innermost thoughts secret from her, and she always had this pervading sense of being married to a stranger.

But then there were times when he lavished her with expensive gifts and told her she was beautiful and the only woman he had ever really loved. During those moments, the passion was ignited between them and they would share long, lingering kisses. It always disturbed Charlotte that there were these occasions when she could feel so madly in love with him and yet not know who he was. She felt as if she was always a little unsure…on the back foot as her emotions swung from one extreme to the other. The pendulum of their love affair was both an exhilarating rush and a terrifying ride.

But throughout those years Charlotte pushed down her feelings of frustration, fear and uncertainty. She learnt how to exist in the shadows in a constant state of denial. Continually, she would tell herself that everything was fine and that all marriages had a few minor concerns. She talked herself into believing that he was a loving husband and would one day make a wonderful father.

For years she tried to have a baby. After the first three years of trying she eventually fell pregnant. But her joy was short-lived. Tragically, the fetus was two months old when she had a miscarriage. Charlotte cried for days but Patrick was strangely detached. She could have sworn he was relieved. So, when she conceived again a few months later, Charlotte was ecstatic. This time she managed to carry the baby to full term. When she gave birth to a beautiful, healthy baby girl she thought her life could not be any more perfect.

But Patrick's strange behaviour towards his daughter was very unsettling. It was as if he was jealous of the time that Charlotte spent with her child. He never seemed to be interested in holding his daughter or getting to know her. As the years passed Charlotte became increasingly aware that Patrick seemed to feel nothing but distain for his only child. No matter how hard she tried she could not seem to get her head around his odd behaviour. It was not natural that he did not seem to love his own offspring. In fact, there were times when she found him to be dictatorial and overbearing with his daughter.

When Elizabeth was three years old, she had been playing in her parent's bedroom. She had stumbled upon her mother's lipstick on her dressing table and decided to draw a picture on the wall. When Patrick walked in on his daughter expressing her creativity, he had whipped off his belt and given her a hiding she would never forget. When Charlotte heard her daughter's screams she charged into the bedroom and wrestled the belt out of Patrick's hands. In that moment, Charlotte concluded she was in fact married to a monster.

It had taken days for the welts and bruises on Elizabeth's chubby little buttocks to fade. The physical wounds healed in time, but the scars were branded into the deepest recesses of Charlotte's soul.

Over the years, Charlotte had carefully watched Patrick's interaction with their daughter. She asked herself if he was capable of real love and if, perhaps, he was devoid of human emotion. He knew how to turn on the waterworks when the occasion demanded it and he was also capable of being affectionate and tender. But Charlotte found herself wondering if perhaps he was a sociopath. She had read once in an article that although these people did not actually feel empathy, they could easily feign it.

On one occasion, after a particularly brutal beating from her husband, she packed her bags and went to stay with her sister in West Sussex. But within hours Patrick has arrived on the doorstep demanding that she come home with him. When she refused, he resorted to blackmail. He told her that he would run away with Elizabeth and she would never see her daughter again. Charlotte had never forgotten the hard steel edge to his voice when he said the words and the menacing look in his eyes. His mouth had curled into a sinister sneer and in that moment, she had felt as if she were staring into the face of the devil himself.

She was too rattled to fight him. Having had the wind knocked out of her sails, she succumbed to him like a delicate flower melting under the midday sun. She went back to her life with him and protected herself and their daughter by walking on eggshells around him. Charlotte watched every word and action to ensure she did not somehow detonate the grenade of his anger. It lurked just below the surface like a crocodile stalking its prey. The smallest intonation in her voice or rising of her eyebrow could set it off.

She learnt to speak to him in silky, honey-coated monotones which lulled him into believing she loved him. Charlotte was careful about keeping a fake smiled fixed on her face to avoid setting his anger alight. The love she felt for him died the day he beat their defenceless little girl. Now, all she felt for him was contempt. Whenever he reached for her in the dead of the night, his breath hot against her neck, she recoiled in disgust. But she always gave in to his advances as an act of survival. Charlotte bided her time, knowing that one day she would find a way to escape his clutches. She would take Elizabeth and start a new life. And, somehow, she would make sure that he never found them.

***

Diane scanned her notes in preparation for the meeting she would be having with her client that morning. Matthew Broadside was the CEO of a large insurance company and had been accused of fraud. He had been caught skimming money from his client's pension funds and if convicted would spend many years behind bars. Diane felt sickened by the whole case. It was clear as day that he was guilty as sin and it would be a challenge to try and get him off. She was convinced it would not be possible. At best she would try and get him a diminished sentence if he pleaded guilty and paid the money back. But the man was stubborn and arrogant and outright refused to acknowledge guilt in any shape or form.

It also did not help that she was struggling to concentrate. Since she had ended her affair with David a few days ago, every thought was consumed by him. She felt like a woman who was trying to go cold turkey from a drug addiction. David's love and attentiveness were a vital part of her life she was not sure she could do without.

She kept thinking about the way her body reacted to him every time he touched her. The feeling of his warm hands against her cool skin was unlike anything she had known before. Even her intimacy with her husband had never reached the heights she experienced with David. It was as if he could read her every thought and knew exactly how to respond to her. The kisses they had shared on so many occasions were branded into her mind almost as if they belonged there. If only she could have shared this intensity of passion with Jeremy. That was all she had ever wanted. In the early days they had fiercely loved each other, but then one day Jeremy had seemed to simply stop listening to her. It was as if something had occupied his mind and she had been pushed out. Diane knew that it largely had to do with his ambition and the fact that he poured so much of himself into his work. He was a pharmaceutical representative and a very talented salesman. He had recently been made Sales Director for the whole of the United Kingdom. So, his work kept him away from home for weeks on end. And, when he did return, he was usually buried under a pile of orders for hours.

Diane tried hard to be understanding. The recession had claimed their home two years ago and Jeremy blamed himself. As a result, he had decided that he would work like a Trojan until he could buy another home. But Diane found herself wondering what the point was when it was at the expense of their marriage. She could not care less about owning a home anymore. All she wanted was her husband's time and attention.

She glanced at her watch and was suddenly consumed by the need to speak to Jeremy. She had a few minutes to spare before the meeting. Picking up her mobile phone, she dialed his number and waited for him to pick up.

'Hi, love,' he said. 'It's not like you to phone me in the middle of the morning. Is everything alright?'

'Yes, Jeremy…everything is fine. I just wanted to hear your voice, that's all.'

'Oh, that is sweet, Di. How has your day been so far?'

'It's been good…I am about to go into a meeting with Matthew Broadside.'

'Is that the guy who swindled all the pension money?'

'Yes, the very one.'

'Sounds like a seedy character to me. Good luck with the case.'

'Hmm, he is a bit dodgy. There is so much evidence that he took the money, so this case is going to be a challenge of note. I have told him that all I am likely to get him is a diminished sentence.'

'Well he has the very best on his side. You know I think you are the cleverest attorney ever.'

Touched by his words, Diane smiled.

'Sweetheart, I know you have to go to the Midlands this week but when you return, we really need to spend some time together.'

'Yes, I know Di. I promised you as soon as I come home, we will go out to dinner. I will take you to the Indian restaurant you love so much.'

'That would be fantastic.'

'I've got to go now,' Jeremy answered. 'I love you.'

Diane's eyes filled with tears. 'I love you too.'

Jeremy was sitting in his car when he took the call from his wife. Fastidious about being distracted by a call whilst driving, he had pulled over onto the side of the road. He was halfway to the Midlands and was enjoying the drive. It gave him time to get lost in his own thoughts for a while. He loved his work, but sometimes it frustrated him as he was acutely aware that his marriage had been taking a back seat of late. He felt tremendous guilt over the fact that he just was not giving Diane the attention and love that she deserved. It was not that he did not love her. The truth was that he would do anything for her. She was the only woman he had ever really loved. But he was simply battling to get over the crippling guilt he felt over the fact that it was his fault that they had lost everything. He had gone into business with a man who later turned out to be a con artist. Jeremy had ended up losing millions as a result. Diane had warned him against the business venture, but he had not listened to her.

As he drove, it occurred to him that it had been months since they had really had a heart to heart chat. He decided that this would change the minute he got back. There had to be a way that they could go back to those early days when they were so madly in love with one another. They had been married fifteen years and sadly very few of those years had been truly happy ones. Jeremy knew that he had to change the cycle before Diane walked out of his life forever.

As he travelled through the narrow country lanes, he thought about all the ways he would make it up to her. He accelerated as his car climbed a hill. Feeling elated, he pushed hard on the pedal and raced down the hill. Suddenly, he noticed a truck attempting to overtake on the corner. The driver clearly had not seen him. He swerved the car and hit the brakes. At the very last second the driver saw him, and his face contorted in shock and horror. There was an almighty crash and then silence.

***

Charlotte unlocked her front door and stepped into the cool interior of her semi-detached house. Her cat, Sebastian snaked his furry body around her legs as she walked down the hall. She scooped him into her arms and smiled as his purr reverberated through his body.

'Are you hungry, my boy?' She asked her voice marinated in affection. 'Let us see if I have a tin of tuna for you.'

Sebastian jumped out of her arms and starting meowing almost as if he understood what she was saying.

'You are so impatient, Sebastian.'

She opened her pantry and reached for the tin of tuna at the back of the cupboard. Opening a kitchen drawer, she located the tin opener and quickly used it to cut open the lid.

Deliriously high on the scent of fish, Sebastian began to meow incessantly. Charlotte deposited the contents of the tin into his bowl and then filled the kettle with water.

She made herself a cup of Earl Grey tea and then walked into her lounge. Since Patrick had been gone it was strangely quiet in her home. It felt both unsettling and peaceful and she knew it would not last.

Easing her aching body into her much-loved chair, she rifled through her handbag until her fingers found her mobile phone. She dialed Diane's number and then lay back against the soft cushions with a sigh. She had the awful feeling of impending doom and she needed someone to talk to.

'Hi Charlie, how are you?' Diane's voice was upbeat and breathless as if she had been running up a flight of stairs.

'Hi Di, I am not too bad.

'Are you sure you're OK? You don't sound good Charlie…'

'It's Patrick – I'm not sure if I want him to live or die at this stage. I just feel like I am in limbo.

The line grew silent for a couple of seconds. Charlotte could hear a sharp intake of breath on the other end.

'Of course, you feel torn, Charlie. It is completely understandable. The man tried to throttle you for goodness sakes. I am sure your emotions will be all over the place right now. Perhaps you can talk about your mixed feelings when we get together for the next 'Apples of Gold' meeting tomorrow night.'

Yes, I do need to talk about it with the group. Di, I want you to know that I will always be grateful to you for saving my life. Thank God you all arrived when you did.'

'We still need to celebrate your birthday, Charlie. The champagne is chilling in the fridge. I will get in touch with the rest of the clan and make a date. How does that sound?'

'Wonderful, thanks Di. I always feel better once I've spoken to you.'

Charlotte turned the taps on full blast and then poured a capful of bubble bath into the water. As she undressed, a cold chill raced down her spine. She shivered in the deepest recesses of her soul. There was no doubt in her mind that Patrick would have a sinister plan for her should he survive. He would be so enraged that he had been attacked in his own house. She stepped into the bath and lay back savoring the feel of the silky, warm water against her skin.

Again, she considered packing a bag and going somewhere far away. But it would be pointless as Patrick would hunt her down and find her. She was sure of it. Charlotte decided she would take her chances and stay where she was. This was her home and why should she be chased from it.

She closed her eyes and fell into a deep sleep where she dreamed of a world where she was free of Patrick and happiness was a reality, not just an illusion.

Patrick very rarely acknowledged her existence let alone thanked her for doing something for him. She walked upstairs and turned down the blankets in the guest bedroom. She had slept there for years and had even resorted to locking the door at night. On too many occasions Patrick had drunk too much and then forced himself upon her. So, to avoid being raped by her own husband Charlotte carefully constructed a world where she could exist, for now.

***

Diane packed up the papers which littered her desk and shoved them into her briefcase. She glanced through the last of her emails and then turned off her laptop. It had been a grueling day and she was looking forward to getting home. She slotted her laptop into her briefcase and stood up. The wall behind her was filled with various credentials and accolades. Diane was an astute and accomplished attorney and her dedication to the law and insight into human nature drew many clients.

She walked out of her office and closed the door behind her. Standing in the hallway waiting for a lift she found herself thinking about Jeremy. The last time he spoke to her he had been unusually warm and tender. It had been many years since he had conversed with her in that manner and she missed it.

As she stepped out into the cool night air a chill settled within her. For a second, she had the sense of impending doom. She tightened the belt of her thick cashmere coat and dug her hands into her pockets. But for some reason her teeth still felt on edge. Walking briskly down Regent Street she dodged the masses of rush hour commuters. She jogged down the steps to the Underground and sighed as she watched the doors of the train slam shut. Standing on the platform, she massaged her temples to get rid of the headache which had begun at the base of her skull. Another train pulled in and she quickly jumped on to it and slumped into the nearest seat. The train lurched and Diane closed her eyes. She was bone achingly tired and relished the idea of a hot bath. Twenty minutes later the train pulled into her station.

Reaching her house, she unlocked the door and walked into the kitchen. She deposited her briefcase on the kitchen table and poured herself a glass of wine.

Diane flopped into the chair closest to the fire and put her feet up on the coffee table. For some reason it felt as if this day had been excruciatingly long. She checked her watch and wondered why

Jeremy was running late. After dialing his number, she waited as it rang in her ear and then went to voicemail.

Her thoughts were interrupted by the sound of her doorbell. Diane got up and walked towards her front door. She opened it to find two policemen standing on her doorstep.

'Mrs Stevens, I'm Constable Evans,' said one of the men extending his hand. She shook his hand warily.

'How can I help you?' she asked her voice rising in concern. The policemen looked at each other. They appeared nervous and on edge.

'May we come in Mrs Stevens?'

Diane nodded and stepped away from the door so that they could enter.

'Yes, of course.'

The men walked into the lounge and then turned to face her. Constable Evans shifted uneasily under her gaze.

'I'm afraid we have some bad news.'

'Is this about my husband?' Her voice shook with raw emotion.

Constable Evans nodded.

'Your husband was involved in a car accident. I am so sorry to have to tell you this…he was pronounced dead on arrival at the hospital. His car is a right off.'

Diane's knees crumbled underneath her. She gagged as the bile rose into her throat.

Constable Evans was immediately at her side.

'Please sit down, Mrs Evans. This is a lot to take in.'

Diane sunk gratefully into the chair and began to sob. It seemed inconceivable that this could have happened. Surely Jeremy would walk through the door any time now. He could not possibly be dead. She shook her head. How on earth would she come to terms with losing her husband?

The tears coursed down her cheeks as the two men stood watching her, uncertain how to help. Constable Evans pulled up a chair and sat down next to Diane.

'Are you alright, Mr Stevens,' he asked gently. Diane was moved by the stranger's warmth.

Suddenly she felt extremely tired and sapped of all her energy. She stood up and began to walk towards the front door.

'Thank you for coming to tell me the news.'

Diane waited for the men to step through her front door and then closed it gratefully.

She stood with her back against the door for the longest time. How strange that her life seemed to have suddenly skidded to a grinding halt at such a fast pace that she was still trying to catch her breath. Surely it could not be true? How could her husband be gone? It was inconceivable. She sank slowly to the floor as the tears began to flow. A million memories flashed across her mind taunting her and pulling at the edges of her already frayed nerves. Diane cried and cried until it felt as if there were no tears left inside of her.

***

Tiffany brushed her teeth vigorously and then spat into the basin. She looked wearily at her reflection in the mirror. Her eyes were red rimmed and bloodshot from crying. She could not help but wonder if there would ever be a day when she would not wake up crying. It felt as if everywhere she went there were reminders of the child she would never hold and whose life she had snuffed out because of her own stupidity and selfishness.

She did not even blame Jason anymore. It had been her decision to abort her unborn child and no matter how misguided she had been she took full accountability for it. She splashed her face with water. There was no more time left for tears. She needed to somehow scoop up the remnants of her broken life and piece them back together like fragments of a fragile vase. There had to be a way she could move on and put the past behind her. But, somehow no matter how hard she tried she would hear the cries of her child in her dreams.

Tiffany's drastic loss of weight only highlighted her high cheek bones and full mouth. Since the abortion she had struggled to eat anything, and it was not surprising she had lost an alarming amount of weight. She felt like a fragile little boat on a turbulent sea. Directionless and lost without a rudder to give her any sense of direction. She found herself wondering if she would always feel this way. Her arms ached to hold the child she had lost. There were times when her emotions were so overwhelming, she could barely breathe. She took one last look at her pinched face in the mirror and then raced down the stairs. It was past nine and she was already late for work. At least she would be able to immerse herself in her most enjoyable pastime once she arrived at the little florist that she owned on the corner of King and Sutton Street.

Jason had been very supportive of her venture and for a few years she had blossomed under his care and encouragement. He had helped her secure a loan to start her business and seemed so committed to their future life together that it was strange how he had run for the hills as soon as a baby was involved in the picture. Their romance had not turned out to be the fairy-tale she once thought it was.

The tube ride to Stamford Brook station was uneventful as usual. The train was packed tighter than a sardine can but thankfully Tiffany had managed to find a seat near one of the doors. She allowed the motion of the train to lull her into a troubled and dreamless sleep.

With a start, she woke up as the intercom announced the train's arrival at her stop.

She stepped off the train into the biting cold and quickened her step. Her shop was a mere ten-minute walk from the station. Tiffany considered herself one of the lucky ones who could honestly say she loved her work. 'Eden Flowers' was her pride and joy and the reason she got up every morning. She loved the fact that she could immerse herself in every flower arrangement she did. No two flower designs were ever the same. She took an enormous amount of pride in her originality and fresh approach. The shop had been open for two years and already in that time she had built a name for herself. She received orders from all over the country and sometimes internationally.

Tiffany unlocked the door of her shop and smiled as she was embraced by a multitude of different scents. Roses, lilies, freesias and the eucalyptus for foliage all combined to offer up a sweet and rich perfume.

The back orders were beginning to pile up and she would need to get through her work quickly today. She needed to do a large bunch of flowers complete with a hamper for a baby shower, a punch of red roses for an anniversary and table settings for a charity lunch. It was a fundraiser for abused children, and they had chosen sunflowers and tiger lilies.

She quickly checked her stock to make sure she had enough of all the required flowers and then she rolled up her sleeves and got to work. As she added to the arrangement flower by flower, it slowly began to take shape. As the sex of the child was not yet know she used butter yellow roses, delicate with a gentle, soft scent. She added in a few white Barberton daises and then tied a massive yellow ribbon around the bunch. On her walk home she had stumbled across the cutest little pair of hand croqueted yellow and white booties, so she had bought them on impulse and placed them in the basket nestled between the roses and the daisies. She signed with satisfaction. It was truly breath-taking.

***

The Apples of Gold support group meeting was in full swing when Jessica arrived late. She had been in two minds about whether to go or not but eventually decided she desperately needed to see her friends.

Diane had phoned earlier that day to tell her about her husband's death. It was just too terrible for words and she knew that her friend would need a lot of support to help her come to terms with it.

'Hi, Jessica,' said Susan. 'Lovely that you could join us. You haven't missed too much we were just getting started.'

Jessica nodded and then smiled weakly. She slumped into the only empty chair in the circle.

'We are just going around the room to find out how the last couple of weeks have been for you all. Diane, let's start with you. I am so deeply sorry to hear about the loss of your husband. How are you coping?'

'Thank you, Susan.' Answered Diane.

'I must admit, I am still in shock. She reached for the box of tissues on the table in the centre of the circle and began to dab at her eyes.

'During our last meeting, I told you all about my affair. It felt so good to get it off my chest and I had decided to end it and tell Jeremy about it. But now I will never have that opportunity as he has gone. I am absolutely consumed with guilt…'

Susan nodded. 'Go on. Tell us some more about your feelings right now.'

'I can't help but wonder if I am somehow responsible for the car accident. I feel it is my fault as I was betraying him, so God took him from me. I know it must sound ridiculous, but I feel like I'm being punished.'

'Oh Diane, it's not your fault. You need to forgive yourself for having an affair. That way you will find healing and begin to grieve for your husband in a healthy way. Are you ready to forgive yourself?'

'Yes, Susan you are right. I know I need to do that. I just don't know how…'

'Well, the first step is to bring God into the equation. You need to confess your sin of adultery and ask for his forgiveness. Then you need to forgive yourself and ask God to help you in your time of grieving. He is faithful and he will get you through this.'

'After the meeting, I will lead you in a time of prayer and you can start the process of healing.'

'Thanks Susan, that would be great.' Said Diane.

'God can also set you free from the chains of sexual abuse which I will also discuss with you later. It means choosing to forgive the perpetrator which is not easy. Don't worry, we'll take it one step at a time.'

'Yes, it will need to be a slow process as that's the only way I'll cope, I think.' Said Diane softly. 'Anyway, that's enough about me. I'm sure someone else would like to share.'

'Charlotte,' said Susan, 'is there any more news about your husband's condition?'

'He's had the surgery, but he is still critical. He's in a coma and the doctor is not sure if or when he will wake up,' said Charlotte.

'How are you feeling? Asked Susan.

'Numb, the love I had for him died a long time ago.'

'I can only imagine,' said Susan. 'But with God's help you can find freedom from domestic abuse and move on with your life. But it will involve forgiving your husband. Do you think you can do that, Charlotte?' Susan asked gently.

'Yes, in time I could do that. Just not today,' Charlotte said shaking her head.

'I understand and I won't push you. You can only take the step once you are ready.'

'Yes, but I do want to start concocting a plan to leave him, should he recover from his head injury. I will need to move somewhere far away and change my name too. It will be the only way to break free from him. I've tried so many times in the past and each time he hunts me down and threatens me.'

'You may need to take drastic measures to escape from your husband,' said Susan. 'But the important part is for you to always remember that you are not alone. God is with you and he will give you the strength to do what you need to. I am praying for you and I believe you will be able to find a way through.'

'Thank you, Susan. I appreciate your support.'

'Jessica, how are you doing?' Asked Susan.

'Still very raw. I keep expecting to see my little Amy bounce into the room. I cannot seem to let go of her. Craig and I are barely talking but we have an appointment with the counsellor tomorrow.'

'It's still very early days in your grief and it takes time. I am glad to hear you are both going for counselling and I hope you can salvage your marriage. Men cope with their grief by burying it, which is not always healthy. Women are usually more able to express their pain which helps.'

'That's all we have time for today. Let us close in prayer.

Father God, thank you for this time that we have had together and for the courage of all the women here. Please fill each person here with your peace and assurance that you are in control. Thank you that no hurt is too big that it cannot be healed. Holy Spirit, please come and fill us. Help us to always remember your consuming love for us, in Jesus name. Amen.

***

Jessica shifted uneasily in her chair. The penetrating stare of the counsellor was starting to unnerve her. But she was determined to continue with the sessions for the sake of her dying marriage. Ever since Amy's death, Craig had just shut down and no matter how hard she tried she could not seem to reach him. He had immersed himself in his work and seemed to survive simply by going through the motions of life in a robotic sort of way. Jessica was particularly concerned as she had not seen him shed a single tear. It was as if he was devoid of emotion. It had taken weeks of begging and pleading to convince him that they needed to see a therapist. He looked tired and haggard but at least he had agreed to see the counsellor.

During the first appointment Craig just sat in his chair, silent and unresponsive. Jessica had done most of the talking. It was now their second session and she was desperate for a breakthrough. There was a solid wall between them and no matter how hard she tried she could not connect with him. It broke her heart to see him so downcast almost as if he had lost the will to live.

The counsellor, Claire had explained that it would take some time to coax Craig out as he had barricaded himself to cope with the magnitude of his loss and guilt. In the meantime, she focused on helping Jessica with her grief but gave her full assurance that she was confident they would be able to reach Craig eventually.

Claire cleared her throat.

'Craig, how are you feeling today?' She asked with compassion in her voice.

The dam finally burst its banks.

'How do you think I feel, Claire? I am responsible for my little girl's death. I am a broken man, utterly gutted and so angry with myself! Tell me Claire, how can I ever get over what I have done? I not only let Amy down, but I've let my family down too!'

Frustrated tears rolled slowly down his cheeks. He squeezed his eyes shut and then sniffed.

‘Craig, I know it feels impossible at this point, but you must forgive yourself. It will be the first step towards your healing.’ Claire shook a tissue out of the box on her desk and handed it to Craig.

‘Look at me, I’m a blubbering mess.’

‘It’s good to cry Craig, it’s the only way you will get in touch with your grief and find healing.’

‘I just don’t know how to get past the guilt, Claire. You say I must forgive myself but how on earth do I do that? I just don’t know…’

‘It takes time and I can assure you that if you keep coming to these sessions and manage to deal with your emotions, you will eventually get to a place where you are able to forgive yourself. What happened to your daughter is an unspeakable tragedy and I can only imagine how broken you must feel. But there is a way through. It takes courage to come here for counselling and you have made the first step. Go easy on yourself and give it time. Your pain is still very fresh, and you still have a long way to go.’

‘I can’t imagine ever getting to the stage where I’ll be able to forgive myself, but I guess you are right. I need to give it time.’

Jessica squeezed Craig’s hand.

‘We’ll get there together, my darling.’

***

Abigail jumped onto the treadmill and cranked up the speed. She was feeling tired and irritable as she had not slept well the night before. But she was determined to have a good work-out for the sake of her sanity. Instinctively, she knew Richard was lying to her about the affair and that is exactly what made the situation so much worse. If only he could be honest with her then at least she could try to salvage the tattered remains of her marriage. But the more he kept secrets from her, the increasingly isolated she felt. The words *see you later darling* was impossible to erase from her mind. For a moment, she wondered if perhaps Jessica was just one of those over exuberant gushy women who called everyone darling. But the moment was short-lived as Abigail felt in her gut that there was more to it than that. She had noticed that Richard was paying more attention to his appearance than he used to, and he had even lost a little weight. She had initially thought that he was just on some sort of health kick, but now his odd behaviour was starting to make sense.

By the time Abigail finished her workout she was drenched in sweat and her heart rate was through the roof. She had pushed herself especially hard today to try and outrun her demons. Not that it had helped much as she still consumed with anger.

She left the gym and unlocked the door to her car. The cool interior seemed to welcome her and for a few seconds she leaned back and closed her eyes. The overwhelming sense of betrayal that she felt was crippling and she could barely breathe under the weight of it. If Richard was not going to tell her the truth, then she would bide her time and catch him in the act. In the meantime, she had to somehow function for the sake of her children. Abigail drove home in a fog of unbridled resentment. How could Richard do this to her? They had always had a good marriage. Or, so she thought.

As she arrived home, she decided to push all the negative thoughts out of her mind and focus on the day ahead. Julie, her au pair had been watching Benjamin and she was grateful for the help. Abigail opened her front door and walked through to the lounge. Her face lit up when she saw her son playing Lego with Julie.

'How's my big boy?'

Spotting her walking towards him, Benjamin ran as fast as his short, chubby legs could carry him. He thrust himself into her waiting arms.

'Mummy, I missed you.'

'But, sweetheart, I was only gone for an hour.' Abigail replied with a warm smile. She held him tight and basked in the scent of his shampoo. He was a delightful child and she was enjoying his toddlerhood and all the benchmarks it brought with it. She was grateful she had been able to spend the first couple of years of his life at home. Abigail had been there for all the crucial stages of toddlerhood. She had caught him as he took his first steps and had been there to hear him try to string a sentence together. Going back to work part-time had not been as much of an ordeal as she expected. She had quickly fallen into a routine that worked. Of course, having Julie to help her also considerably eased the pressure.

For a moment she held her son in her arms and tried to pretend that everything was just fine and that her husband was not having an affair. She felt as if the bottom had fallen out of her world and the betrayal simmered within her like the glowing embers of a dying fire.

***

For the longest time, Tiffany simply stared at the handful of sleeping tablets she had poured out of the bottle into her lap. She just wanted so desperately to go to sleep and never have to wake up to the pain. It was killing her. She struggled to eat and had become dangerously thin. Jason had not been as supportive as she had hoped. Instead, he almost seemed to resent her for the overwhelming grief she was feeling.

Her friend Julia had just given birth to a baby girl. But Tiffany could not even bring herself to go and visit the baby. It was just far too excruciatingly painful to be anywhere near babies. She felt as if her heart and soul were ripped apart and nothing could put them back together again. Tiffany only felt a small measure of reprieve when she knocked herself out with sleeping tablets and feel into a deep sleep. But even then, her dreams were invaded, and she would wake up wide eyed and haunted by the terrible thing she had done.

How could she have been so stupid? Why hadn't she put more thought into the consequences of what she was doing? She should have carried the baby to full term and then given it up for adoption. But she had been so scared and simply wanted to please Jason. And then he had given her an ultimatum.

How could he? She found herself thinking that there was something cruel and heartless about Jason. Although he promised he would marry her and they would have children together, a nagging feeling in her gut told her otherwise. He had been so distant and disinterested lately. Every night he would come home from work and sit and watch the telly drinking beer after beer. The routine was always the same…Tiffany stayed in bed crying until she felt as if her heart would burst, and Jason would simply watch TV. With crystal clarity she remembered their conversation the night before.

'Tiff, you have to stop this. You need to let go. It's all in the past now.' Jason had perched on the side of her bed and stroked her forehead.

'It's not that simple Jason. I cannot move on. How on earth do I forgive myself for what I've done?'

Jason shook his head. 'Stop beating yourself up, Tiff. We did what we thought was necessary under the conditions. Please…I hate seeing you like this.'

It was the first time Jason had spoken about what they had done on that terrible grey, cold morning. For months he had acted as if nothing had happened and carried on with life as usual.

Today she had felt so depressed she could not even get out of bed. She phoned her assistant at the florist and said she was ill and would try to make it in tomorrow. But Tiffany did not want there to be a tomorrow to this hell of a life she was living. If she were to die, she would be reunited with her baby…she would hold her baby in her arms and she would be just where she was supposed to be…with her child.

To take the edge off the enormity of what she was about to do, she poured herself a glass of wine and quickly swallowed a handful of sleeping pills. She relished the appealing thought that within a few minutes it would all be over. There would be no more pain or regret. She would finally be free of the heartbreak and the dark stain on her soul.

Tiffany pulled her duvet over her head and closed her eyes. At such a time as this her faith kicked into action and she began to say the Lord's Prayer. *Our father, who art in heaven, hallowed be thy name…*

***

Jessica knew she was on a dangerous and slippery slope. One lie had turned into two lies and before she knew it, everything she said to her husband seemed to be a lie. Even before the affair had started, Craig and Jessica had been oceans apart. The distance between them seemed insurmountable since Amy's death. It was clear they were grieving in different ways. Craig was blaming himself as was Jessica but of late she had found refuge and a brief respite in the arms of another man. They had met at a business conference just a few weeks before the drowning. Jessica had thought many times about ending it but the deep resentment she felt towards her husband stopped her every time. The stolen moments she spent with Richard were like a soothing balm to her tortured soul. Every time she so much as looked at Craig the events leading to her daughter's death played like a stuck record in her mind. If only her husband had taken his duty seriously instead of engrossing himself in a rugby match. If he had done what was asked of him their little girl would still be alive.

Jessica did feel a small remnant of compassion towards Craig as she knew he was being eaten alive by guilt and she told herself she would not add to it. But even the counselling sessions they were going to every week did not seem to be helping much. There was just too much anger and pain between them. They could not reconcile the enormity or what had happened that fateful day, no matter how hard they tried.

Jessica was grateful for the warmth and companionship she had found in the friends she had made through the Apples of Gold support group. She had been astounded by how much they all had in common. Each woman carried painful secrets, the burden of which had been halved in the sharing of them.

***

Upon arriving at Tiffany's house, Jessica walked up the garden path and then knocked on the door. She knew Tiffany was at home as she had spotted her car parked on the street.

With no answer from the inside, she knocked again.

'Hi Tiff, it's me, Jess.' She called. An uneasy feeling began to settle over her. Jessica turned the door handle and finding it open she walked into the house.

'Hello'...

She walked into the lounge area and then the kitchen but there was no one there. Jessica turned and walked up the stairs. Tiffany's bedroom door was closed. She tapped gently on the door. 'Tiff, may I come in?' she said tentatively.

After a few seconds, Jessica opened the door and walked into the bedroom. Tiffany was lying in her bed and appeared to be sleeping. Jessica walked towards her slowly. 'Tiff, wake up sweetie.'

She sat down next to her friend and shook her gently. 'Wake up, Tiff.'

Her heart skipped a beat when she noticed an empty medicine container on the bedside table. She sucked in a breath as she read the label. Zopiclone was a sleeping pill she was familiar with as she had used them herself in the past.

Adrenalin shot through her as she realised, she needed to act fast. She reached for her mobile phone and then called 999. Hopefully, the paramedics would arrive quickly. She checked Tiffany's pulse. It was weak but she was still alive.

Please help me God, she prayed.

Once she was sure the paramedics were on their way, she scanned her contacts list in her phone to find Jason's number. Her hands shook as she held the phone to her ear.

'Hello,' Jason said.

'Hi, Jason its Jessica. You need to get home now. Something has happened to Tiffany.' She could not get the words out quick enough.

It was clear he had been drinking as his words were slightly slurred. 'What? OK, I am leaving now. I am just at a work function. What's happened to her?'

'I think she's taken an overdose of sleeping tablets. I popped in to visit her, but I have not been able to wake her. She is unconscious but still breathing. I have called 999 and the emergency services are on the way. Jason, I think she took the whole bottle, so I am really scared. Just get here as soon as you can.'

'Right, I am on my way Jess… just catching a cab and should be back in about thirty minutes if the traffic is not too hectic. Thank God you found her Jess. I'd hate to think what could have happened if you hadn't.'

'I'll phone you as soon as the paramedics arrive.'

'Thanks so much, Jess…'

She ended the call and tried to wake Tiffany again.

'Tiff, wake up please…'

***

It took just fifteen minutes for the emergency team to

Jessica's call. They descended on her semi-detache

into her bedroom. John, the paramedic in charge took hei r

was faint.

'Thank God, you're here,' Jessica said her eyes filling with tears.

She handed the empty medicine container to John. 'Here, this is the medication I think she took. I have no idea how many...'

'We have to rush her to the hospital and get her stomach pumped. It's not a good sign that she's lost consciousness.'

John's partner helped him to ease Charlotte onto the stretcher. He strapped an oxygen mask to her face.

'Right, let us go.'

Jessica stood up. 'May I come with you?' she asked tentatively.

'Of course, if you wish mam.' John replied.

Once they were safely in the ambulance Jessica reached across and grabbed Tiffany's hand. 'I'm here, Tiff. You are going to pull through this. Please just hang on sweetheart.'

Within a few minutes they arrived at the hospital. The doors to the emergency wing of the building flung open and staff streamed out eager to help. Jessica got out of the ambulance and followed the stretcher inside. John was suddenly beside her.

'Mam, you are going to have to wait here. You can't go any further.'

'I understand,' Jessica replied.

'Why don't you go home and get some rest? If you come back in the morning, I'm sure the doctor will be happy to speak to you then.'

Jessica nodded. Suddenly, a feeling of acute exhaustion swept over her. She slumped into the nearest chair in the reception area. Her mobile phone started to vibrate in her pocket. Jason was trying to call her.

'Hi Jason,' she said with a tired sigh.

'Is she alright?' He asked with panic in his voice.

'I'm at Hammersmith Hospital.' Jessica replied. "They're pumping her stomach and told me to come back in the morning to speak to the doctor. The paramedic said it's not a good sign that she's unconscious.' There was silence on the end of the phone for a couple of seconds as Jason struggled to get the right words out.

'Go home, Jessica. I'll come to the hospital now and you can come back in the morning.'

'OK, Jason. Do you want me to wait until you get here?'

'No, I'll be fine. Just go home and we can chat tomorrow. But if I do have any other news before then I will give you a call.'

'I need to let the others know. I just feel like I do not have the energy to call them right now. I'll wait until I get home.'

'Good idea' He paused. 'Thanks again for all your help. You're a true friend…your quick thinking saved her life.'

'I had a hunch that something was wrong as we hadn't heard from her for a few days.'

'Yes,' Jason replied. 'She has been very low for months now. But I didn't know just how depressed she was…'

'You and me both, Jason.'

'Well, she's in good hands now.' Jessica said.

'Bye, Jason…I'll speak to you later.'

Jessica sighed as she stepped onto the train which would take her home. It was congested and she was not in the mood to deal with crowds of people. She walked through the carriage until she eventually found a seat in the corner next to a window. Sinking gratefully into it she leaned back and closed her eyes. It occurred to her that Craig must be wondering where she was. She had been so consumed with helping Tiffany that she had completely forgotten to contact her husband.

She looked at her phone and notice she had a missed call from him.

Inhaling a deep breath, she called his mobile phone.

'Jess, are you alright? I've been worried' Craig said.

'Sorry, Craig…I've had a very taxing day. I will explain when I get home. My train is on time, so I'll be there in half an hour.'

'Great, Jess. I've made dinner and Beth and I have both eaten so you don't need to worry when you get home.'

'Thanks, that's so kind of you.'

'You sound tired.'

'I'm exhausted, Craig. It has been quite a day. You will not believe how challenging it has been. But I'll tell you all about it later.'

Jessica placed her phone in her handbag and leaned back. What she would not give to be in a steaming hot bubble bath right now. The day's events swirled around her head like a black mist. Tiffany had tried to end her life. It was just too much to take in. She sniffed and reached for her tissue as a lone tear escaped and rolled down her cheek. Maybe it was time for her faith to be ignited again. Gone were the days when she used to pray every day. The day she had lost Amy, Jessica had shut her heart to God. She blamed him for taking her baby girl. Although she knew this decision was not helping her, she was not sure what else she could do. No matter how hard she tried, she just could not seem to bring herself to really reach out to God. She was just so incredibly angry inside.

She felt as if her heart and soul had been shattered into a million pieces. There were well meaning friends who told her that time heals all wounds. Well, she certainly did not find that to be true. The intense pain she felt was overwhelming every day. All that time had given her was the simple ability to keep functioning regardless of her hurt. She was grateful she had Bethany to keep her going. Since losing Amy there had been moments when she had contemplated taking her own life. But the thought of leaving Bethany without a mother motivated her to get out of her bed every morning.

Her thoughts turned to Tiffany. It gave her a small measure of comfort that even though she was not able to save her daughter from drowning; she had at least managed to save her friend. Jessica's heart filled with compassion towards Tiffany. She completely understood the deep ache she felt over the loss of her baby. She wished she had known Tiffany when she had the abortion. If they had been friends, perhaps she would have been able to talk her out of it. Now it was too late. The damage had been done and Tiffany had tried to end her life. Jessica felt resentment towards Jason rise within her. How could he be so cruel?

***

Tiffany opened her eyes and then squinted at the harsh overhead lighting. She looked around the hospital room warily as her eyes filled with tears. How had she possibly survived? She was so sure she had swallowed enough sleeping tablets to kill her.

Jason walked into the room carrying a huge bunch of flowers.

'Tiff, how are you feeling, love?' He stroked her forehead gently.

'What were you thinking?'

Tiffany began to sob. 'I just can't take the pain anymore, Jason. It just hurts too much.'

Jason sat down in the chair next to the bed and took his hand in his own. He squeezed her fingers gently.

‘I’m so sorry, Tiff. I feel as this is my entire fault. I have been so absorbed with work I have not paid you enough attention. I almost lost you…’

He climbed into the bed next to her and took her in his arms.

‘It’s going to be different from now on,’ he said tenderly. ‘I promise you.

But I do think it is time you spoke to a professional about how you are feeling. What do you think?’

Tiffany nodded her head as Jason handed her a tissue. She blew her nose and then turned to face Jason.

‘Do you love me?’ she asked.

‘Yes, of course I do,’ Jason replied.

‘Then why do I feel so alone in my pain? Her voice was barely a whisper.

‘We both agreed to the abortion, but I feel as if you don’t support me in the grieving process.’

‘I suppose men and women simply deal with their pain differently. I know I have not expressed it much, but I am also battling to come to terms with it. But we made the right decision at the time. You know you are too young to have a child.’

Later that day, Diane, Charlotte, Abigail and Jessica walked into the hospital ward bearing gifts. Jessica burst into tears when she saw that Tiffany was awake.

She walked over to her friend and pulled her into an embrace. The compassion and warmth she experienced birthed a fresh flood of tears and Tiffany began to sob.

Feeling uncomfortable by such an elaborate show of emotion between the women, Jason climbed off the bed and addressed them.

'I'm just going to nip out to get a coffee. I'll leave you to spend some time with Tiffany.'

'Thanks Jason,' Diane replied.

Tiffany received hugs from each of the women and eventually her tears subsided.

'How did I get here?' She asked.

'All I remember is taking the sleeping pills.'

'I popped into your house on my way home, Tiff.' Jessica answered.

'Thank God I found you just in time. I called the paramedics and they rushed you here. You had your stomach pumped and you were in the Intensive Care Unit for twenty- four hours. We almost lost you.'

Diane reached for Tiffany's hand. 'Please, you need to talk to us about how you are feeling. You are going through a grieving period and you need your friends.'

'I know you are right, Di. It is just that there has been so much going on in all our lives and you've just lost Jeremy, so you are also grieving. I didn't want to burden you all.'

'Yes, we all have a lot going on, Tiff.' Abigail said her voice gentle and reassuring. 'But that doesn't mean we can't be there for each other.'

Tiffany nodded. 'I'm sorry for putting you through more pain,' she said.

'Just promise us you won't do it again,' Diane said. 'They'll take good care of you here in the hospital and I believe a psychologist is coming to see you this evening. I'm not a doctor but I do think it would be a good idea to consider going onto anti-depressives for a while…just for a few months until you start feeling better.'

'Yes, I will talk to the doctor when he comes in,' Tiffany replied.

Tiffany turned towards Jessica. Again, her eyes filled with tears. 'Thanks so much for finding me, Jess. I do not really want to die…it is just that I cannot live with the pain anymore. But that is enough about me.'

***

Jessica was exhausted and every muscle in her body was crying out for relief. Now that the adrenaline rush had subsided, she was feeling dreadfully tired. She closed her eyes and prayed *thank you Lord for saving Tiffany.*

It had been a long and exhausting day and she was desperate to get into a hot bath and wash off the clinical hospital smell which seemed to linger in her nostrils.

The day had simply been insane. Tiffany had tried to take her own life. Jessica felt as if her entire world was falling apart. The loss of her precious baby was so painful that most days she could barely get out of bed. Each day was a painful reminder that her beautiful little angel was no longer with her. Then there were the problems she was having with Craig. He was just so distant towards her and never wanted to talk about Amy. Jessica knew that he was wrestling with terrible guilt, but she just wished she could reach him somehow. The drowning had happened months ago and yet it felt like yesterday.

Jessica's mind wandered towards the man she was having an affair with. He had been so kind and supportive towards her and she wondered if she was falling in love with him. She felt an element of guilt, but this was quickly eclipsed by the resentment she felt towards Craig for not taking his duties seriously in taking care of Amy on that horrendous day. She was not sure their marriage would be able to survive the tragedy. They could barely even talk about it without becoming embroiled in a heated argument.

Then there was her relationship with God to consider. Prior to the drowning Jessica and Craig had faithfully attended their local Presbyterian Church every Sunday. Jessica served on the team looking after babies in the Mother's Room and Craig helped with the sound equipment. They had been attending the church for five years now and they were happy there. Jessica wondered how she could possibly have fallen so far from grace. Now, not only had they stopped attending church since Amy died, but she had also gotten involved with a married man. She knew that at some point she must make peace with God and ask for his forgiveness. But, right now all she could manage was to simply breathe and exist day after day. She would push herself to keep going for the sake of her other daughter. Bethany was at such a vulnerable age and desperately needed her support.

Arriving at her home she walked quickly up the garden path and opened the front door. She walked into the foyer and placed her handbag on the table in the passage.

'Hello, I'm home,' she called. Bethany raced down the stairs.

'Hi mum, I'm so glad you're back. What a hellish day you have had. Tell us all about it.'

Craig walked into the room and pulled her into a warm embrace. 'How are you doing?' He asked with compassion. Jessica was surprised by his sudden warmth.

'I'll tell you all about it. Beth, please make me a cup of tea. I'm gasping here.'

'Sure Mum, coming right up.'

Jessica hung up her coat and then walked through to the living area and collapsed on her sofa. She removed her shoes and then tucked her feet underneath her. Craig sat down next to her. He had some important news to tell her but now was not the right time. Knowing it would be better to wait; he turned his attention to his wife.

'How is Tiffany doing?'

Jessica sighed. 'She is still very low, but I think she is relieved to be alive. I think the suicide attempt was a cry for help. Craig, she is in so much pain over the abortion. We really need to try and help her somehow. I am going to speak to the counsellor at our church. I have heard that she's excellent.'

'Yes, Jess. That sounds like a good idea. I knew you would be tired, so I've ordered pizza for tonight, so you don't have to cook.'

'Oh, that is so kind of you, Craig. I want to just go and soak in a hot bath. I have been at the hospital for most of the afternoon and evening.'

Bethany walked into the lounge and handed her mother a hot cup of tea. 'There you go, mum.'

'Thank you, my darling girl.' Jessica stroked the cheek of her precious child and then turned to walk upstairs.

She turned the bath taps on full blast and then poured bubble bath into the water.

Stepping into the water, she immediately began to relax. She lay back and watched the frothy bubbles pop around her. Sipping her Earl Grey tea, she willed her mind to switch off. Never had she felt so utterly emotionally and physically drained. But one thing she knew for certain was that to find her way through this complicated maze she found herself in, she needed God. It was time to forgive Him for taking her beloved Amy and get real with him about her feelings. The only time she ever truly felt safe was when she was in the presence of God.

God, I need you. I forgive you for taking my beloved Amy. I know she is safe with you. I am so scared right now and so worried about Tiffany. Please look after her Lord. Help me to end the affair with Richard. Forgive me for wandering so far away from you. I need your mercy and grace, please Father. I pray all of this in Jesus name.

Jessica immediately felt convicted that she needed to break off her affair with Richard. She would go and visit him the next day and then would put her heart and soul into repairing her marriage. 'I forgive you Craig,' she whispered. Immediately she felt as if a weight had been lifted off her.

***

Jessica had locked herself in the bathroom to make the call to Richard. He agreed that they needed to end the affair. Now that she had dealt with that she would talk to Craig about their marriage and how they could save it. She quickly got dressed and padded softly down the stairs. Craig was cooking one of her favourite meals, Carbonara with ample garlic and cheese.

'Smells wonderful,' she said with a smile.

'I thought you would enjoy it after the kind of day you've had, Jess.'

'Thank you, Craig. That's very thoughtful of you.'

'Bethany has gone to the movies with her friends so it's just to the two of us tonight.'

'How lovely,' Jessica replied.

Jessica laid the table and then opened a bottle of wine, a full-bodied Cabernet. Craig dished up the food and then brought the plates to the table. Jessica sat down and placed her napkin on her lap. Craig took his seat at the end of the table and for a few seconds there was an awkward silence between them.

'Jess, there is something important I need to talk to you about. I know the timing is not great considering recent events, but I can't put it off any longer.'

'Oh really, what's on your mind?'

'Well, you know things have been strained between since we lost Amy. We are both dealing with our grief and we've shut each other out but we can't go on like this.'

'I know Craig. That is why I booked the counselling sessions.'

'We've been several times now and I feel that we are not getting anywhere.'

'Jess, I've thought very long and hard about this and I think there is only one solution.

I want a divorce…'

***

Diane had worked a fourteen-hour day and she was beyond exhausted. She checked her watch. It was ten fifteen and her bed was calling her. Turning off her laptop, she rose from her desk and straightened her skirt. At least working late delayed the inevitable loneliness of walking into an empty house. She missed Jeremy desperately and on this day the sense of loss she felt was acute.

She turned off the office lights and walked towards the elevator. Once inside she sighed and closed her eyes. The welfare of the girls was on her mind and she wondered how Jessica and Abigail's visit with Tiffany had gone. Diane would have loved to attend as well but she had just been far too snowed under with urgent cases requiring her attention.

The lift took her down to the basement where her car was parked.

But as she stepped out into the dimply lit car park, the hairs on the back of her neck stood on end. Was she being followed? She slowly turned around and scanned the car park. There was no one to be seen.

She walked over to her car and just as she was about to open the driver's side door a dark shadow crossed her path. A man placed his hand over her mouth. She felt the hard metal of a gun pressed against her ribs.

The man's face was concealed under a balaclava. For a second, she looked into his black, sinister eyes. There was familiarity about them that she just could not place. Was it possible she knew him?

'Get into your car.' He said, spitting out each word.

With her heart in her throat Diane did as she was told.

'Good, now lie down across the passenger seat.'

The man leaned over her and ripped open her white blouse. Then he pushed her skirt up and pulled down her underwear. Diane desperately tried to wriggle away from him. Terrified, angry tears escaped from her eyes.

'I have been waiting for you…' His breath was hot and stale.

Diane wept as flashbacks of the abuse she had suffered as a child infiltrated her memory.

The man unzipped his pants and then rammed himself into her. Harder and harder, until Diane was sure she would be bruised internally. He kept the gun pressed hard against her head and she was sure it was going to go off any minute. Sheer terror overwhelmed her.

'Consider this a warning.' He said with malice in his voice.

He kept the gun on her as he slowly stepped backwards. Step by step until he darted through the doors which led to the road outside.

Adrenaline shot through Diane. Her mind could barely comprehend what had just happened to her. She started her car and headed in the direction of her local police station.

All the suppressed emotions of anger and pain of her abuse as a child had resurfaced and now, she had been brutally raped. The words her attacker had spoken to her kept running through her mind. *Consider this a warning…* The words sent cold shivers down her spine. For a few seconds she had thought he was going to kill her after he raped her. Why had he let her live? Was it some sort of a game he was playing? It was obvious he knew her.

Diane felt as if her very soul had been ripped clean out of her body. For years she had tried desperately to put the pieces back together, but the truth was she was broken, fragmented and tormented over the abuse she had suffered. Red hot anger burned within her. She had felt so helpless and afraid. The violation she felt was all consuming and she wondered how she would make it through this devastating experience. She stopped her car on the side of the road and gave full vent to all the emotions she was feeling. Diane sobbed and sobbed. How could this happen to her so soon after Jeremy's death It was just too much to bear.

Diane dried her tears. She was a survivor and somehow, she would get through this. She buttoned up her jacket to conceal her torn blouse and continued her drive to the police station.

Arriving there, she climbed out of the car and walked slowly to the entrance. The warm interior of the station welcomed her and for a second, she felt a little less alone in the world.

***

Because she had attempted to take her own life, Tiffany was on strict suicide watch at the private psychiatric clinic she had been admitted to. Already a week had passed, and she was feeling no better than she did prior to taking the overdose. She was heavily sedated, and she found her daily sessions with her doctor tiresome.

'How are you feeling, today?' Dr Bennet asked.

'I'm still feeling very depressed,' Tiffany answered as her eyes filled with tears.

'Tell me about your feelings. What is going through your mind right now?'

'I wish I could go back and change what I did. I can't seem to forgive myself for aborting my own child.'

'I understand,' Dr Bennet replied. 'It will take time to heal.'

Tiffany reached for a tissue on the coffee table and then blew her nose.

'Will I ever stop feeling so terrible?'

'Well, I have doubled the dose of your anti-depressive medication so that should start to kick in soon.'

'Jason has been acting very strangely lately,' Tiffany remarked.

'I don't think he can handle the fact that I'm in a nut house right now.'

'Well, I wouldn't call it that, Tiffany. You need to look at it from a different perspective. You are here to get well. It is a safe and secure environment and you have doctors, nurses and counsellors on hand to help you get there. How do you feel about the group therapy? Is it helping at all?'

'A little,' Tiffany answered. 'I have met some really nice people and it does help to connect with others suffering from depression. I feel there is no judgement there, just acceptance which is very comforting.'

'That's good to hear.' Dr Bennet nodded as he scribbled on his note pad.

'I also enjoy the art classes…'

'It's all part of the therapy we offer here, and I am so pleased to hear you are making such good progress. You may feel as if nothing's changed, but I can see that you are a little better than you were a week ago.'

'How long do you think I need to stay here?' Tiffany asked.

'For as long as it takes to get well, my dear.' Dr Bennett took off his glasses and rubbed his eyes. 'It all depends entirely on you…'

Tiffany nodded. 'Well, I am trying my best to get well.'

'Remember that it is important to just take it one day at a time. I know you are feeling weak and vulnerable right now, but you will not always feel that way. The sessions with your psychologist will also really help you.'

'Can I go now, doctor? I'm feeling really tired.'

'Yes, of course. I will meet with you again tomorrow then.'

Tiffany attempted a weak smile and then got up and walked out of the room.

She spotted another one of the patients walking towards her.

'I'm going for a fag outside. Do you want to join me?' Charmaine asked throwing her arm around Tiffany.

'Yes, I think I need one after my session with Dr Bennett.'

'Ah, yes…I know exactly what you mean.'

'It's just that he comes across a little patronising at times. He tells me he understands how I feel but how on earth could he possible know what it's like?'

'Well, you know…all those years of training makes him a professional at prescribing head medication for us.'

Tiffany laughed. 'Charmaine you are such a card. I'm so glad I met you.'

'Me too, Tiffany.'

Charmaine opened the door to the small garden outside and as the women stepped out into the sunshine, for a moment all their worries were forgotten.

Tiffany lit a cigarette and then inhaled deeply. She blew the smoke out gently enjoying the way it felt in her mouth.

'How are you doing today, Charms?'

'Fine, I guess. I have my good days and of course there are the inevitable bad days.

Charmaine had attempted suicide as the voices told her to. She did not seem to mind that she had been diagnosed as a paranoid schizophrenic. Free spirited and unassuming, she wore her label almost with pride. She had grown up in the East side of London and sported several tattoos and a nose ring. Her long, auburn hair was tied up in a messy ponytail and her large, blue eyes always appeared startled.

Tiffany had instantly warmed to her. Regardless of her colourful personality and off the wall antics, she was a caring, kind individual whom she could instantly relate to.

When Tiffany had been admitted to St Johns Psychiatric Clinic, she was initially appalled to discover she would have to share a room with three other women. But after a few days of Charmaine's constant chatter and friendly overtures, she succumbed to her charm and they were soon sharing midnight candy bars, whispering like little children in the darkness so the nurses would not hear them. The fact that one of the other women snored was a constant topic which had them both indignant and exhausted from lack of sleep. Tiffany and Charmaine had complained about it to the head nurse, but nothing was done. So, they had embarked on a campaign to be moved to another, less noisy room.

'Are your friends coming to visit you today, Tiffany?'

I am not sure, will just have to wait and see.'

Charmaine had met Diane, Jessica, Charlotte and Abigail and had instantly warmed to them. They too were taken with Charmaine's laid-back attitude and sunny personality. It was a comfort to know that Tiffany had found a friend in the clinic.

***

Jessica, Abigail, Charlotte and Diane were pleased to be reunited at the Apples of Gold Support Group. So much had happened during the past two weeks and they had a lot to catch up on.

Abigail noticed that Diane was looking particularly fragile. Her usually glossy blonde hair was limp and dull, and her skin was ghostly pale.

Whilst they were waiting for the other ladies to arrive, the three women started talking amongst themselves.

Jessica noticed that Diane's hand shook slightly in her lap and she appeared disoriented. She reached across and embraced her friend in a hug.

'What is going on, Di? You are not yourself.'

Diane nodded. 'No, I'm not. There is something I need to tell you...'

'What is it?' said Abigail with concern in her voice.

'Last night I worked very late. When I went down to the parking lot I was attacked by a man. He raped me at gunpoint.'

Jessica inhaled sharply. 'Oh, Di that is terrible. Did you go to the police?'

'Yes, I reported it. My attacker had been waiting for me. I did not see his face as he was wearing a balaclava.'

Diane choked back the tears and squeezed her friend's hands.

'Don't worry about me. I will get over this somehow.'

'You're the strongest woman I know Diane,' said Abigail. 'But I am worried about you. First losing Jeremy, then this...'

'I know, Abby. It is a lot to take in.'

Susan walked into the room and closed the door behind her.

'Welcome everyone, I'm glad to see so many of you here this evening. Shall we get started then?'

The eight women in the room nodded in unison.

'Let us open in prayer.'

Father God thank you for each woman who is here with us tonight. I pray that your Holy Spirit will minister to each lady and bring comfort and healing. I pray that you will speak to them from your Word and remind them that they are not alone in their individual journeys. In Jesus name, amen.

'Firstly, ladies…I want to say how proud I am of all of you for coming this evening. I have been in touch with a few of you during the past couple of weeks and I know you have faced some battles which have seemed insurmountable. I heard about Tiffany's attempted suicide. Well done for your quick intervention, Jessica. Thanks to you she is now on the path to healing. I went to visit her at St John's Clinic last week and although she was sedated, she seemed to be a little better. We will keep praying for a speedy recovery.

'I just want to go around the room and find out from each of you how you are doing and what we can pray for.

Jessica, how are you doing?'

'I still feel very raw over the loss of my baby girl. It was the six-week anniversary yesterday and I just fell apart. Then, when I arrived home from work yesterday my husband told me he wants a divorce…'

'I'm so sorry to hear that,' said Susan. Her gentleness reduced Jessica to tears.

'I just can't believe it. We have been going for counselling and I thought we were making progress. But he is just so closed to me. I don't know how to reach him.'

'In my experience as a counsellor, couples who experience losing a child often break up as the pain divides them and they can't comfort each other. But this is not always the case. I have also seen God do amazing miracles and save marriages from the brink of disaster. Do you want to hang onto your marriage, Jessica?'

'Yes, absolutely. I love my husband with all my heart.'

Susan nodded. 'Are you able to truly forgive him for your daughter's death?'

Jessica closed her eyes for a second. 'I really want to, but I just don't know how.'

'I understand,' replied Susan. 'It says in the Bible that we can do all things through Christ who strengthens us. He is the one who will help you forgive Craig. It is not something you can simply do on your own. Are you willing to trust God with this important decision? But before we deal with that, we need to talk about you forgiving yourself for what happened.'

Jessica was suddenly overcome with emotion. She was so moved by the counsellor's kindness and compassion and she knew she needed to break free from the prison she was living in. It was true…she blamed herself more than Craig for Amy's death.

Susan handed her a tissue and Jessica dabbed her cheeks.

'Jessica, do you know Christ as your Lord and Saviour?'

'Yes, I did. But that was before the drowning. I had been a Christian for many years. But when I lost Amy, I blamed God. I am still so angry with him. How could he let this happen? I don't understand…'

'Yes, it is difficult to get your head around why God allowed it to happen. I do not have all the answers. We live in a fallen world full of evil and all I can say to you is that when trouble comes God promises to be there with you in it. He doesn't promise a life free of pain, but he does give us the assurance that he will never leave us nor forsake us.'

Jessica nodded.

'Yes, what you are saying makes sense. I have walked closely with the Lord in the past and its absolute torment feeling so far from him now. I just cannot seem to get past the anger I have towards him. Every time I try to pray the resentment just overwhelms me.'

'I understand, Jessica. That is entirely normal. You have a lot of conflicting emotions you need to work through. But God can help you with the process. That is if you allow him to.'

'I know...I need to let him in again.'

'Are you ready to do that now, Jessica? Do not worry if you feel it is too soon. God is very patient.'

'Well, I just don't want to carry on feeling this way, Susan. It is killing me. I think it's time I started healing with God's help.'

'Wonderful, then let us pray together,' Susan said gently.

***

Jessica drove home from the Apples of Gold support group feeling lighter than she had in a very long time. As Susan prayed for her,

Jessica had chosen to forgive God, Craig and even herself for her daughter's death. Even though she was still in deep mourning and the painful loss she felt was still there, she felt a sense of hope for the first time since she lost her daughter.

Her thoughts turned towards Craig. She dared to hope it would be possible to save their marriage. She was not surprised that he was asking for a divorce. She had been cold and distant with him ever since the drowning. Why on earth would he want to salvage their marriage?

Susan's words played over and over in her mind. *God can turn your marriage around if you let him.* Dare she hope for that? She began to pray, *Please God, save my marriage. I put my life in your hands and pray for the strength to get through this. Thank you for your saving grace. Have mercy on us, please Jesus.*

She pulled into her driveway. As she walked to her front door, she prepared herself for the conversation she would have with her husband. She unlocked the front door and stepped into the passage. The rich aroma of garlic mixed with curry powder embraced her.

Bethany bounded down the stairs.

'Hi Mum,' she said pulling Jessica into an embrace.

'Hi, princess… I do love coming home to a welcome like that.'

'Dad's cooking Thai green curry tonight…I can't wait.'

'Yes, I know you love it Beth. How was school today?'

'It was fine, I guess.'

'That's good. Now go and wash your hands for dinner.'

Jessica walked through to the kitchen. Craig looked up from his cooking and smiled at her.

'Hi Jess, I knew you would be home late so I thought I would cook dinner.'

'That is so kind of you, Craig. I appreciate it so much.'

'No problem…'

Jessica approached him tentatively. 'Can we talk after dinner?'

'Yes, of course,' he answered. 'Dinner will be ready in ten minutes.'

'Is there anything I can help you with?' Jessica asked.

'You can open a bottle of wine if you like?'

'Sure.' Jessica opened the door of the pantry and took out a bottle of Cabernet Sauvignon. She poured a glass for Craig and one for herself.

'Do you mind if I take a quick bath before dinner?' Jessica asked. "It's been quite a long, hard day.'

'Of course, take your time.'

Jessica walked upstairs and turned on the bath taps. As she lay back in the bath, she sipped her wine and reflected on the day. She was so grateful for the Apples of Gold support group. For the first time in six weeks she felt a glimmer of hope that there was indeed a way out of her deep darkness. She still felt so raw inside. Ever since Amy had died, a cavernous hole remained in her heart. Dare she believe that God could fill that hole?

She closed her eyes and began to pray.

Please take my pain, God. I cannot carry it anymore. Thank you that I am not alone in this. You are with me.

A deep sense of peace began to settle over Jessica. She lay in her bath and savored the feeling. Peace had been absent from her life for so long and she was so grateful to finally feel God's reassuring presence.

After her bath she dressed in a pair of jeans and a T-shirt. She knocked on Bethany's bedroom door.

'Honey, dinner is ready.'

'Thanks, mum. I am coming now.'

Jessica walked down the stairs and into the kitchen.

She took a seat at the dining room table and smiled as Craig brought her a plate full of food.

'How lovely to be served like this,' she said.

Craig squeezed her shoulder. 'I know it's been a rough couple of days for you, Jess.'

Bethany sat down at the dining room table.

'It smells delicious, Dad. I am so hungry.'

'Well, here you go,' said Craig handing her a plateful of food.

The family ate in silence and once the dinner was finished, Jessica collected all the plates and loaded them in the dishwasher. Bethany returned to her bedroom to finish her homework.

'Craig, that meal was so tasty. Thank you so much.'

'It's a pleasure, Jess. Glad you enjoyed it.'

'Craig, let us talk about why you want a divorce.' Jessica said softly.

'Jess, we just cannot carry on like this. We are so far apart from each other. There is no intimacy between us anymore. I feel guilty every time I look at you as I know you blame me for Amy's death.'

Craig's eyes were brimming with tears. 'Jess, I just can't take it anymore. I figure that if I divorce you; I will set you free from having to look at me every day and feel the disappointment and loss.'

Jessica reached across the table and squeezed his hand.

'Craig, I blame myself and even God for Amy's death. But today at the Apples of Gold support group I chose to forgive myself. I feel so much better and I am experiencing a peace that I have not felt since we lost Amy. I guess at one point I did blame you. I really am sorry, please forgive me. I don't want to lose you too.'

'I don't want to lose you either Jess but perhaps if we are apart, we will be able to heal. I wish so desperately that I could go back and change everything. If only I had watched Amy. I should never have asked Bethany to do it. I berate myself about it every day and I just can't stand the torment anymore.'

'Craig, you need to forgive yourself. It is the only way you will find real freedom. You walked closely with the Lord before we lost Amy. You can find him again.'

'Jess, I'm just so angry at God. How could he have allowed this to happen to us? I just don't understand.'

'Neither do I. There are some questions I guess we will never have answers to. But one thing I do know is that God is good, and he is with us. He feels our pain and he wants to help us. But he can't help unless we invite him in to do so.'

Craig nodded. 'Yes, I know you are right. I just feel so broken and cannot seem to find any hope right now. Do you really think our marriage has a chance?'

'I do, but only with God's help.'

'Please don't give up on us,' Jessica whispered. 'We need each other, and we must fix our marriage for Bethany's sake. She has gone through so much loss already. I don't want her to experience the devastation of a divorce too.'

'OK, Jess…but please be patient with me as I am such a mess inside.'

'I understand, Craig. I love you and I want our marriage to be saved.'

***

Even after scrubbing herself thoroughly in a hot bath, Diane still felt dirty. The events from earlier kept replaying in her mind. How was it possible that she had been brutally raped by a man who seemed to know her?

iane knew that the only way through this would be to call ›ng-forsaken faith. She lay back and began to pray. The words of Psalm twenty-three came to mind.

Be still before the Lord and wait patiently for him; do not fret when men succeed in their ways, when they carry out their wicked schemes.

The words sank deep into her spirit and a sense of peace settled over her. The Bible had been a source of comfort to her ever since she first gave her life to Christ when she was twenty-four years old. She had found healing and comfort from the horrors of her childhood but during the past couple of years she had been so focused on her career that she had wandered away from God. But Jeremy's death had brought her back to her knees and she knew the only way she would survive now was with God's help. She realised that God was telling her to wait for him. This was something which seemed almost impossible to do as her thirst for revenge grew stronger by the minute.

The police had not been much help. The problem was that they saw so many rape victims that perhaps they had become a little complacent. They had said they would investigate it, but Diane did not have much confidence in them finding her attacker.

She decided that tomorrow she would make it a priority to go and visit Tiffany. The girl needed as much support as she could get during this very painful time of her life.

Lord, please give me strength, she prayed. She had never felt so alone and scared as she did right now. Jeremy had been her anchor and safe place and now he was gone. All she had left was her faith in God.

Because he loves me, says the Lord, I will rescue him. I will protect him, for he acknowledges my name. He will call upon me, and I will answer him; I will be with him in trouble, I will deliver him and honour him.

The scriptures God breathed into her broken spirit immediately warmed and comforted her. She was not alone. Her Saviour was with her and he would help her to fight the battle. He would give her the wisdom and strength she needed. For the first time in many years Diane felt a deep assurance that everything would work out.

Visiting Tiffany would present a unique opportunity for Diane to talk about God. Tiffany needed her encouragement. God had been speaking to Diane about her friend and she knew that she would play a vital part in Tiffany's recovery.

Diane checked her reflection in her bathroom mirror. She applied a coat of mascara to her lashes and put on her red lipstick. Right now, she needed as much courage as she could muster. She walked downstairs and out into the bright spring sunshine.

There was time for contemplation during the long drive to the clinic. Diane had many of her own demons to overcome. The rape kept playing over in her mind.

Diane parked her car and then walked into the clinic. The receptionist looked up.

'May I help you?' she asked.

'Yes, I'm here to see Tiffany Stevens.'

'That's fine; she should be in the common room now. You can go through.'

'Thank you,' replied Diane.

She walked into the lounge area and scanned the room looking for Tiffany. As it was visiting hours the room was a hive of activity. She spotted her friend at the back of the room helping herself to a cup of tea. Diane walked quickly towards her.

Tiffany looked up and smiled.

'Hello Di, what a lovely surprise,' she exclaimed with a smile lighting her face.

'How are you, darling? Are you feeling better?' Diane asked.

'Let us sit down and we can chat,' replied Tiffany.

The women walked over to one of the sofas which would afford them a little privacy.

'It's so good to see you, Di.' Tiffany remarked as she sipped on her tea.

***

Jessica was becoming increasingly worried about Bethany. Her daughter had been acting very strangely for weeks now and had taken to dressing like a Goth. She only wore black and painted her nails in the same colour. Jessica felt as if she was losing a second daughter to the heavy metal music which blasted from her room all hours of the day and night. Craig had tried to convince Jessica that it was just Bethany's way of dealing with the death of her little sister.

'I think it's just a phase, Jess. Try not to worry about it too much. She will grow out of it.'

'I'm not so sure, Craig. I am worried she is getting worse. She hardly says a word to either of us anymore and she is hanging out with the weird crowd from school. I have heard they all do drugs so I am very concerned that Beth might be on drugs too.'

'I know you are concerned, Jess. But remember what Claire told us at our last session. She said we must just continue to love and support her regardless of her behaviour right now. Bethany needs to feel safe, not condemned.'

'I know but I just feel so helpless that I can't reach her. She is in so much pain and it's hard for me to just stand by and watch her struggling so much.'

'Yes, I know but we have asked her if she wants to see a counsellor and she said no. We have to respect her wishes and not force the issue.'

'I know you are right, Craig. It is just so hard.'

Jessica sniffed as warm tears inched down her cheeks.

Craig pulled her into an embrace. Gently he stroked her hair.

'It's just all so hard.' Jessica whispered.

'It will get easier with time,' replied Craig.

'I still feel as raw as the day she died.' Jessica sobbed.

'I just want my baby back! And, now I feel like I am losing my other child. It's just too much.'

'I understand, Jess. I know it is agonising. I feel the same way. All we can do right now is take it one day at a time. Just put one foot in front of the other and keep going for Bethany's sake. She really needs us to be strong right now. And, when the time is right, she will let us in.'

'How can you be so sure?'

'I just feel it in my gut. She does not really want to be alone in all of this. She is just trying to make sense of it all. We are all just trying to survive this unbelievable tragedy.'

'I need to pack up Amy's room, but I just can't seem to do it…'

'That can wait until you are ready, Jess. Remember Claire said you cannot rush the grieving process, and everyone grieves in different ways. Let us just leave Amy's bedroom as it is for now. I also can't bear the thought of packing up her things.'

'I keep expecting her to walk through the door full of sunshine and light.'

'Me too…'

Jessica wept until she felt as if she had no more tears to cry. She felt broken and empty. There was a huge hole inside her heart that only her baby could fill. Somehow, she had to let go, but at this stage it felt like an impossible task.

She felt a measure of comfort in her husband's arms and was so grateful that they had managed to salvage their failing marriage. For the first time since she had lost Amy she felt as if Craig was grieving with her. For many weeks he had withdrawn from her and shut her out completely. But since going to the grief counsellor they had managed to find each other again. She knew that the key lay in forgiveness and she had truly done this. She did not blame Craig for the death of her daughter. She had grace and mercy for him. Jessica did not blame Bethany either. Instead she blamed the one who in her mind should have saved her precious daughter. Her soul raged with anger as he should have been there and was not. He could have prevented the drowning of her child and yet he did not. There were so many questions which screamed at her in the dead of the night when sleep evaded her. Why God, why?

What terrible thing had she done to warrant her losing her darling child? How could God have watched the tragedy unfold and yet done nothing to prevent it? Jessica's mind could not grasp how this awful blow had been inflicted on her family especially as she had spent most years of her adult life following and serving God. She had been a Christian all her life and had grown up in the church. But now she felt that in her hour of need God had let her down. The loneliness in her soul was amplified a hundredfold by the total desolation she felt over her belief that God had not been there for her. When she needed him most, he had failed her? How could she find it in her heart to forgive him?

Craig on the other hand had found comfort through turning to God. Jessica admired his unshakable faith and wished she could feel the same way. But, no matter how hard she tried, she could not seem to get past the emotions that engulfed her every time she thought about God. She felt betrayed and alone.

Jessica had met with her Pastor to discuss her feelings towards God. Michael had explained that God does not promise us a life free of pain but instead he does give us assurance that he will be with us in trouble. But these words fell on deaf ears. Jessica did not want to hear trite religious words whilst her grief was still so raw. How could Michael possibly understand what she was going through when he had never had the misfortune of losing a child? She had politely excused herself and said she would speak with him again in a few months once she was feeling a little better. But that day never came. Today she still felt naked and vulnerable. Every breath she took hurt and she wondered if she would ever feel normal again. The pain she felt was all consuming and nothing helped to ease it.

Deep down in her heart she knew that the only true solution would be to forgive God and turn back to him. She knew instinctively that she would find comfort in him. But she just did not feel ready to let go of her anger. Perhaps it was just easier to hate God and blame him for what happened instead of believing in a loving and gracious God who understood her pain and could heal her wounds. She closed her eyes for a minute as a scripture came to mind.

The Lord will surely comfort Zion and will look with compassion on all her ruins; he will make her deserts like Eden, her wastelands like the garden of the Lord. Joy and gladness will be found in her, thanksgiving and the sound of singing.

For the first time since her daughter's death, Jessica felt an assurance that she would find her way through her pain. Regardless of her bitterness towards God, he had spoken to her and comforted her with his promises. She began to sob as she was overwhelmed with the true nature of the God, she had followed all her life. Even though she had turned from him and blamed him for the tragedy, he still pursued her and found her in the deepest recesses of her tortured soul.

***

Finding out about Richard's affair had knocked the wind out of Abigail's sails. The fact that he was still choosing to lie to her galled her and made her feel estranged from him. Instinctively, she knew he was having an affair no matter how much he chose to deny it.

This morning she was hosting a mom's and tots' group at her house in the hope that it would take her mind off all her troubles. She had finished displaying all the toys on her lounge carpet and the stage was set for what should be an enjoyable morning. There were two mothers she had met at her church who would be joining her, and she was looking forward to relishing a little adult company. She adored her son Benjamin but sometimes the days alone with him were lonely and she missed adult conversation.

She finished unloading the dishwasher and placed the teacups on a tray. Reaching into the fridge she took out her freshly baked chocolate cake and took it through to her lounge.

As if on cue, she heard a knock at her front door. She opened the door and hugged her friend, Annie. Abigail had met Annie at her church only a few months ago but already the two women had formed a strong bond with many shared interests. Annie had brought her toddler twins who played well with Benjamin as they were the same age.

‘Come in,’ Abigail said with warmth in her voice.

‘It’s so lovely to see you, Abby. I bought some cookies I baked yesterday.’

‘We are going to have so much food as I also baked a chocolate cake.’

The women walked through to the lounge and settled the children on the floor. Benjamin started to build a house with his Lego blocks and the twins played with their dolls.

There was another knock on the door and Abigail rose to go and answer it.

‘Hi, Cathy…I’m so glad you came.’

‘Thanks, Abigail; it’s great to see you.’

Cathy walked into the lounge carrying her three-year old son, Justin. It was the first time Cathy had brought her son over to play with Benjamin and the women were hoping the two toddlers would get on.

‘Do you like cars and trucks, Justin?’ Abigail asked. ‘We have lots of exciting toys here for you to play with.’ Abigail walked into the next room and arrived carrying a plastic box packed full of toys. She took out some trucks and placed them on the floor next to Justin. Benjamin eyed him warily.

'Annie, this is Cathy. I am not sure if you have met her at church yet. She has only just joined a couple of weeks ago.'

'Pleased to meet you Cathy,' Annie said.

The children played contentedly on the floor whilst the women sipped on their tea. Abigail wished she knew the women well enough to confide in them about her troubles, but she thought that now was not the right time. Perhaps she could ask Annie to join her tomorrow for a time of prayer and she would tell her then. It was draining trying to put up a front and appear happy when inside she was shattered. Instead she smiled and conversed with the women and simply basked in the sense of fulfilment she had in being around adults for a change.

Abigail had given up her full-time job to focus on raising her family. She knew how important it was to be around for her children especially in their most formative years. It was fortuitous that Richard earned enough so that she could stay at home with their children. But on some days, particularly because of Richard's affair, the loneliness felt overwhelming. Richard worked very long hours. When he returned home in the evenings, he usually ate dinner and then went straight to bed. Abigail had very little time with him and it grieved her. Although her days were busy, for months now she had longed for more interaction with her husband.

She had already decided that she would confront him again about the affair. This time she would not give up until he told her the truth. Weeks had passed and he had just swept the whole matter aside as if it were not important. Every time she asked him, he simply said he was not having an affair. But Abigail had spent ten years being married to Richard and she knew him probably better than he knew himself.

There were a few minor squabbles amongst the children over some of the toys, but tactful intervention solved the problem and they went back to playing happily. The day was warm and bright, so the women ventured into the garden to make the most of the April sunshine. Finally, after a long, cold winter it seemed spring had finally arrived. The children raced outside and were soon bouncing on the trampoline and then riding on their scooters.

Cathy mentioned that she needed to get going as she had to take Justin to a dentist appointment.

'Justin, come here. Let us put on your socks and shoes.'

The little boy climbed off the trampoline and ran towards his mother.

'Abigail, thank you so much for inviting us over to your house. Justin had fun and I really enjoyed the company too.'

'It's a pleasure, Cathy. You are most welcome anytime. We will do it again soon.'

Cathy picked up her son and walked towards the door.

'I'll see you on Sunday then. Annie, it was lovely to meet you.'

'Great to meet you too, Cathy.'

Abigail closed her front door behind Cathy and walked through to the lounge. She picked up the teacups and cake plates and put them on the tray. Then she walked towards the kitchen. Annie followed her into the kitchen.

'Abby, is everything okay?' She asked gently. 'I've noticed that you are not yourself today.'

Abigail sat down at the table in her kitchen and burst into tears. Immediately her friend was at her side.

'What's wrong?'

'Where do I begin?' whispered Abigail. 'So much has happened and it all feels more than I can bear.'

She took a deep breath. 'I think Richard is having an affair.'

'Oh, Abby I am so sorry to hear that.

You are carrying so much pain alone. I'm your friend and I want to help you.'

'Thanks Annie, your words mean a lot to me. I so appreciate your thoughts. Please just keep me in your prayers.'

'Of course, I will. I am here for you. Why do you think Richard is having an affair?'

'I found a note in his pocket. It said *see you later darling!* And it is not just the note that is a red flag. He has also been acting very strangely. He has revamped his wardrobe and started running suddenly. I confronted him about the affair, and he said he is not being unfaithful. But Annie, I can feel it in the pit of my stomach. I just know that he is lying to me.'

***

Diane swallowed the rancid bile rising in her throat. She had been feeling ill all morning and she had an important meeting coming up in just a few minutes. So far, she had managed to keep the nausea at bay by sipping on Ginger Beer, but it was clearly getting worse. She stood up from her desk and then grabbed the corner to steady herself as her knees buckled beneath her. She wondered if perhaps last night's Chinese takeaway was the reason for this sudden onslaught of ill health.

She gagged as the vomit rose in her throat. Diane only just made it to the office toilet where she purged her stomach of its contents. The room tilted slightly as dizziness engulfed her. She felt marginally better since she had thrown up her breakfast. She splashed some cold water on her face and checked her reflection in the mirror. There were dark shadows underneath her eyes and her complexion looked grey and washed out. Diane had not felt this ill since she was pregnant with her first child. But the pregnancy had ended in a miscarriage at just seven weeks. She had been heart broken and although Jeremy and Diane had tried for many years to conceive a child, it had not been possible.

Diane knew that that was the reason she threw herself into her work. Whilst she was consumed with her job it kept the demons at bay. But now she had lost Jeremy so there was no hope of her having another baby.

It occurred to her that perhaps she had fallen pregnant when she was raped. The thought made her shudder. *Please God no*, she prayed.

But the nagging thought that it could be possible hounded her. Her menstrual cycle was already a few days late, but she had not been too concerned. She had recently turned forty and had assumed her late period was possibly early onset menopause. But she would have to do a pregnancy test to find out. At least then she could put her mind at rest.

She buttoned up her jacket. Somehow, she would get through the meeting.

Diane walked into the board room and shook hands with her client. Steve Johnson had reason to believe that one of his employees had been embezzling funds from his construction business. It was up to Diane to build a strong case against the perpetrator. He had been very careful in covering his tracks, so she really had her work cut out for her. She somehow managed to endure the hour-long meeting but as soon as it was over, she raced to the bathroom and vomited again.

There was no way she could stay at work whilst battling the crippling nausea and vomiting.

She walked over to her secretary's desk.

'Rosie, I'm not feeling well so I'm going home. Please reschedule all my meetings for the day. If I feel better later, I may try to do some work from home.'

'Yes, of course,' Rosie replied. 'I must say you look very pale, Diane.'

'I'll be fine. I will stop at the pharmacy on the way home and pick up some anti- nausea medication. I had Chinese takeaway for dinner last night so maybe that's given me food poisoning.'

'I hope you feel better soon.'

'Thanks Rosie. Hopefully, I'll see you tomorrow.'

Diane was relieved that the train journey home was uneventful. She even managed to find a seat as it was outside of rush hour. She leaned back and closed her eyes for a second. The rape replayed over and over in her mind. Surely, she was not pregnant? But what if she was? What would she do? Diane did not believe in abortion so that was not an option.

She got off the train at Victoria station and starting walking towards her home. She knew there was a pharmacy on her route, so she planned to go in and buy a pregnancy test.

The pharmacist was very helpful and handed her a pregnancy test which would give accurate, fast results.

Arriving home, she walked up her garden path and unlocked her door. Her heart was hammering in her chest and her head felt like it was held in a vice. She took a couple of pain killers and then walked into her bathroom. Sitting on the toilet her fingers shook as she took the pregnancy test out of the box.

She read the instructions and then did the test. The next few minutes were grueling as she waited for the results. Diane felt so ill she was sure she would faint any second. She vomited again and sat down on the cool, bathroom floor and began to pray. *Please help me Lord; I am so scared right now...*

Immediately a sense of peace settled over her. A scripture came to mind. *Though the mountains be shaken, and the hills be removed, yet my unfailing love for you will not be shaken nor my covenant of peace be removed, says the Lord who has compassion on you.*

Diane knew that regardless of the test results she would be able to face her future with confidence. God had given her a promise and she knew that he was with her.

She inhaled and reached for the plastic stick. Turning it over she gasped. The test was positive. Diane's eyes filled with tears. How on earth could she give birth to a child that was conceived through a rape?

For a few minutes she sat on the floor and cried until she felt certain her heart would break. She struggled to make sense of everything.

She continued to pray until she felt God's peace settle over her once again. She knew deep in her spirit that she was not alone.

***

Finding out about her husband's affair had completely unhinged Abigail. She felt as if her world was falling apart around her.

Abigail decided that she would not let up on Richard until he had told her the whole truth about his affair.

She was frazzled from another busy day with her fussy toddler and mountains of laundry.

With a sigh she folded the last of the laundry and packed it away in her children's bedroom.

Benjamin was fast asleep, and Sophie was watching Winnie the Pooh on television. Richard would be home in a few minutes and Abigail had decided that once they had eaten dinner and put the children to bed, she would talk to him.

As if on cue, she heard his key turn in the lock. He walked towards her with a huge smile on his face. 'How is my lovely wife?'

He kissed her on her forehead.

For a moment she leaned into him enjoying the scent of his aftershave. Then she pulled away and walked into the kitchen.

'Dinner will be ready in five minutes.'

Richard followed her into the kitchen.

'What's wrong? You are acting very strangely.'

'You know what's wrong, Richard. But I do not want to talk about it now. Let us just have dinner and once the children are asleep, we can talk.'

'OK,' Richard replied with a weary edge to his voice.

Abigail had cooked a Thai red curry with prawns accompanied by a fresh garden salad. The family all sat down to eat dinner.

After dinner, Abigail loaded the plates and cutlery in the dishwasher and then took the children to bed.

'Sophie, give your father a kiss goodnight.'

'Daddy, can you read me a story?'

Richard nodded. 'Of course, I can my little princess. Just a quick one.'

Richard took his daughter's hand and walked with her up the stairs and into her bedroom.

'Which story would you like to read, my angel?'

'Um…I think we should read The Jungle Book tonight.'

'Now that's a good choice,' he answered with a smile.

As she had woken Benjamin for dinner, Abigail was a bit concerned she might have trouble putting him down to sleep again after he had eaten. She made up a bottle and cradling him in her arms she fed him. When he had finished drinking his milk, she gently rocked him, singing lullabies in the hope he would fall asleep.

Eventually his little eyes grew heavy and he fell into a deep sleep. Abigail took him upstairs and placed him in his cot.

She suddenly felt bone achingly tired and was not looking forward to the conversation she would have with her husband.

Richard finished reading The Jungle Book to Sophie and then tucked her up in bed and deposited a kiss on her forehead.

'Sleep well, my princess. I love you very much.'

'I love you to the moon and back, Daddy.'

'I love you more,' replied Richard with a wink.

Richard walked down the stairs and into the kitchen. Abigail was pouring herself a glass of wine.

'Would you like a glass?' She asked.

'Yes please,' replied Richard.

They walked into the lounge and sat down.

'So, what do you want to talk about, Abby?'

'I want you to come clean about the affair. I just know you are lying to me Richard and I need to know the truth. You at least owe me that.'

Richard nodded. 'Of course.'

His shoulders slumped as he exhaled. 'I will tell you everything. Her name is Jessica and I met her at a conference several months ago. Initially nothing happened between us. It was strictly professional. But a couple of months ago we were both working late at the office and it somehow just happened.'

'What do you mean it just happened?' Abigail asked with her voice rising.

'Nothing just happens!'

'Calm down Abby. I am trying to be truthful here. What I am saying is that it was not planned. It just happened.'

Abigail signed. She was losing the battle here. 'OK, go on…'

'She is also married but not happily. About six months ago she lost a daughter. It was a tragedy as she was only four years old. She drowned when Jessica's husband was supposed to be watching her.'

Abigail's heart rate sped up as she began to connect the dots. Was it possible that her friend Jessica was the same woman who was having an affair with her husband? Surely it could not be?

'What is her surname, Richard?'

'Collins…'

Abigail inhaled very slowly as tears filled her eyes. She tried to blink them back, but they escaped and rolled down her cheeks.

'Abby, I'm so sorry. I know this is so hard for you, but I have ended it now. Jessica wants to work on her marriage.'

'Damn it, Richard! Jessica is one of my friends that I met at the Apples of Gold Support Group.'

Richard's jaw dropped as he dissected the news.

He got up and started pacing the length of the lounge.

'I'm so sorry, Abby. Please forgive me. Of course, I didn't know she was a friend of yours…'

'Yes, well she is. Jessica has become one of my best friends! How could you do this to me, Richard? I thought you loved me!'

'I do love you, Abby. You and the kids mean everything to me. Please, it was a mistake and it only happened twice. I was stupid and selfish. I felt like all your time was being spent on the kids and you were always too tired to have time for me…'

'What a load of nonsense! That is a lame excuse, Richard!'

Abigail's mind was spinning as she tried to grasp the reality of the situation. She felt so humiliated by the double betrayal. How on earth was she going to deal with this situation?

'Richard, I can't stand the sight of you right now. I need you to move out whilst I try and process all of this.'

'Surely we can work it out,' Richard bleated.

'No, just get out…'

***

Tiffany had been in the private psychiatric clinic for two weeks and she was losing patience with her recovery. She desperately wanted to go home but she was still very severely depressed and suicidal. No matter how many pills she swallowed or how many sessions with the psychologist she had, she simply could not forgive herself for murdering her unborn child.

Initially Jason had come to visit her every day but of late his visits were becoming less frequent.

She checked her reflection in the bathroom mirror. Her eyes looked sunken and there were deep rings underneath them.

In a few minutes time she had another session with her psychiatrist, so she thought she had better try with her appearance. She applied a little foundation to her skin. Then she put on some eye shadow and mascara. Tiffany immediately felt marginally better.

She left her room and walked down the long corridor to the psychiatrist's office. Dr Bennett was nice enough and he was trying hard to help her.

Tiffany knocked tentatively on the door.

'Come in.' Dr Bennet answered.

She opened the door and walked into the office. Dr Bennet motioned for her to sit down. He was a short, stocky man with a bald head and bushy moustache.

'How are you doing today, Tiffany?'

'I'm OK, I guess.' She answered.

'Tiffany, you have been here for two weeks now and we have spoken many times about the suicidal thoughts that you keep having. I know you are struggling to forgive yourself for the abortion and you seem to be locked in a vicious cycle. I want to suggest something to you.'

'I am trying really hard to get past it, but you are right…I can't forgive myself.'

'Have you ever heard of Electroconvulsive Therapy or ECT?'

'No, I have never heard of that. What is it?'

'Well basically, it is a very effective form of treatment for depression. It involves putting you to sleep for a short period of time with electrodes on your head. Then short pulses of electricity will be applied to your brain. These help you to forget painful memories so that you can heal from the depression.'

'That sounds very hectic! I'm not sure that I want to do it.'

'Well, it is a lot to take in. Here is a booklet about the treatment. Go and read it and give it some thought for a few days. I have treated many patients with ECT, and it does work.'

'I will think about it.'

'Are you sleeping well, Tiffany?'

'Yes, I am thanks. The sleeping tablets certainly help.'

'It is a very effective medication but can become addictive, so I don't want you on it for too long.'

'I know, doc.'

'Have you noticed any difference since we increased your dose of anti-depressives?'

'Not really. I still feel very down most of the time.'

'It does sometimes take a couple of weeks to take effect. We will just have to keep an eye on you.'

'Have you any idea when I may be able to go home?'

'I think you need to stay here for at least the next two weeks, Tiffany. We must monitor the effects of the increased medication. Our time is up now but I will see you again tomorrow.'

Tiffany nodded and stood up. 'Thank you, Doctor.'

As she left the doctor's office Tiffany felt as if she had the weight of the world on her shoulders. She desperately wanted to leave the clinic, but she was still feeling so low. But the thought that Diane was coming to visit this evening immediately lifted her spirits. She would talk to her about the ECT treatment.

Tiffany walked into her room and flopped onto her bed. She only had half an hour to wait until visiting hours and she was impatient to see Diane.

She fell into a deep sleep where once again she dreamed of her unborn child.

About half an hour later, one of the nurses woke Tiffany.

'Your visitor is here to see you.'

Tiffany threw on her jumper and walked out of the room. As she walked into the common room, she noticed Diane sitting on one of the sofas. She stood up as soon as she saw Tiffany walking towards her.

The women embraced.

'Tiff, it is so good to see you. How are you feeling, sweetheart?'

'I've been better' answered Tiffany. 'But it really helps to lift my spirits having you here, Di. I saw my doctor this afternoon and he has suggested that I have Electroconvulsive Therapy. But I am not sure about it. What do you think?'

'I think it is quite a radical form of treatment. But if the doctor has suggested it then perhaps it is an option, but you need to think about it carefully. I think we should ask God what he thinks. He could heal you in a heartbeat. Would you like me to pray for you?'

'Yes, I would like that,' Tiffany answered.

Tiffany was not perturbed by the people milling about around her. She was just desperate to feel better.

'Tiffany, have you ever given your heart to Jesus?' Diane asked.

'I went to church when I was a child, but it never really had much meaning for me. I'm ready now to give my heart to Jesus.'

Diane led Tiffany in the sinner's prayer and then asked for God to heal her from depression and anxiety. Tiffany immediately felt a peace she had never known before settle upon her.

'Tiff, I feel you need to forgive yourself for having the abortion. That is what's keeping you in a state of depression.'

Tiffany nodded her head as a fresh rush of tears poured down her cheeks.

'Yes, you are right, Di. But how do I forgive myself? I just don't know how to do it.'

'God can help you with it. Just trust him.'

'OK, I am going to forgive myself. I know it is the only way to move forward.'

'I feel that God is saying that you also need to forgive Jason for pushing you into having the abortion.'

Tiffany nodded. 'Yes, I do feel very resentful towards him. Di, I feel our relationship is falling apart. He does not come to visit me every day anymore. I am not sure what is going on with him. Maybe it's the end of the road for us.'

'Don't try to figure everything out. God is in control of your life and if you commit to following him, he will direct your steps. It says in the Bible that if you delight yourself in the Lord, he will give you the desires of your heart. Just trust him.'

'Thank you, Di. I feel so peaceful. I really appreciate your prayers. You really are a true friend.'

***

Abigail was so angry about Jessica's betrayal that she could barely breathe. She wondered if she should go around to her house and confront her. No, she did not want to see her. Instead she would phone her to discuss the matter. She kept thinking about all the occasions she had confided in Jessica. Yet, all this time she had been having an affair with her husband. The pain sliced through her and left her feeling exhausted. She was not sure who she was most angry with, Richard or Jessica.

She needed to calm herself before she made the phone call. Pacing the length of her lounge she tried to bring her feelings under control. Sophie was at play school and Benjamin was sleeping so now would be a good time for her to make the call.

Abigail made herself a cup of tea and then reached for her Bible. She knew that it was only with God's help that she would be able to face this awful situation. Turning to the book of Psalms she was immediately comforted by the scriptures. *Because he loves me, says the Lord, I will rescue him. I will protect him for he acknowledges my name. He will call upon me, and I will answer him. I will be with him in trouble; I will deliver him and honour him.*

The peace of God settled over her and she immediately knew that with God's help she could face the future. Admittedly, she was feeling scared and overwhelmed. She was financially dependent on Richard and had two small children to raise. It had been a mutual decision for her to give up work to become a full-time mum. But if she were to divorce Richard, she would most likely have to get a job. There was much to consider and all the thoughts patrolling her mind were giving her a headache.

Abigail looked through her handbag until she located a box of pain killers. She took two and then closed her eyes for a few seconds. As soon as the headache was gone, she would phone Jessica.

The matter needed to be handled with great sensitivity. Abigail felt she could extend grace to Jessica because of her recent loss. She could not even begin to imagine how devastating it must be to lose a child. She prayed that God would give her the words and that she would be gentle regardless of her pain.

With shaking hands, she located Jessica's number on her phone and waited for her friend to answer.

'Hi Abby, how are you doing?' Jessica asked.

'I've been better, Jessica. There's something I need to talk to you about.'

'Sure, what is it?'

'I know about you and Richard.'

Silence hung between them for a couple of seconds. Jessica inhaled slowly.

'I'm so very sorry, Abby. It only happened a couple of times and it's over now.'

'How could you do that to me, Jess?' Abigail said. Her voice was barely a whisper.

'I have no excuse other than I was vulnerable and lost and stupid. Craig and I had not been getting along since Amy's death. You know that. I met Richard at a work function, and he was just so kind and thoughtful and one thing led to another.'

'I don't want to hear the details, Jessica.' Abigail answered with a firm edge to her voice.

'Please find it in your heart to forgive me, Abby. I truly am very sorry. I have been going out of my mind with grief over Amy's death and I guess I just have not been myself. But still, it does not give me an excuse.'

'You need to give me some time, Jessica. It is not easy as it is a double betrayal. It's inconceivable that an affair has happened between one of my best friends and my husband.'

'I can only imagine how you must be feeling. I didn't know he was your husband when the affair started.'

'That does not matter, Jessica. You must have known he was married. He wears a wedding ring and so do you. It's just wrong plain and simple.'

'Yes, of course…you are right.'

'I don't know where to go from here, Jessica. I have to go and fetch Sophie from school now and Ben will be waking up from his nap.'

'OK, Abby. Take care and I hope we can talk again soon.'

'Bye, Jessica.'

Abigail ended the call and put her phone back in her handbag. She could hear her toddler son waking up from his nap, so she walked into his bedroom and gathered him up in her arms. He immediately stopped crying and clung to his mother.

'Are you hungry, little man?' she asked tenderly.

Benjamin nodded.

Abigail walked into the dining room and strapped her son into his highchair. She had just a little time to feed him before she had to fetch Sophie from school. Opening the fridge, she looked for Benjamin's favourite food, mashed butternut.

Benjamin clapped his hands in delight.

Abigail fed her child and then changed his diaper. She was glad that she had him to distract her from the awful thoughts which had been running through her mind. She knew she had to forgive both Richard and Jessica, but it was all just too raw to contemplate right now.

Perhaps in time she would feel less vulnerable and betrayed. She knew that she just needed some space to clear her head and think straight. Her world had been turned upside down and she desperately needed to feel some normality again.

She buckled Benjamin into his car seat and then reversed her car out of her driveway.

The pre-school was close to her house, so it usually took about ten minutes to get there.

Abigail sighed at the roadworks sign on the road ahead. Frustrated that she would now have to wait she turned on the radio and flipped through the channels. Eventually she found some soothing classical music. She allowed it to wash over her like waves of the ocean. Deep in her soul she knew that whatever happened God was with her and she would make it through.

But she could not get the conversation she had with Jessica out of her head. The fact that her friend had been having an affair with her husband just did not seem real. It felt surreal, almost as if it were happening to someone else.

Abigail shook her head in disbelief. She felt like she was living in some bizarre horror movie.

Please God, give me strength she prayed.

***

Diane's bed sheet was wrapped tightly around her from all the tossing and turning she had done the night before. No matter how hard she tried, sleep had evaded her. She kept having flash backs to the horrific rape she had suffered only a few short days ago. It disturbed her that the rapist seemed to know who she was. She had an awful feeling of impending doom. As if he was waiting to come and finish her off.

She decided that next time he came after her she would be ready. Diane walked into her bedroom closet and reached to the top shelf to locate her gun. She picked up the box and placed it on her bed. She had bought the silver pistol many years ago and was proud of the fact that she had taken the time to learn to shoot. Diane decided that today was a good day to visit the shooting range.

She picked up a box of bullets and put them in the box with the gun. It was a cold spring day, so she shrugged on her hooded jacket and walked out into the fresh crisp air.

The shooting range was a twenty-minute drive away. Diane was relieved to find that the range was relatively quiet, so there would be no queuing this time around.

She paid for her session and put on her googles and earphones. She stepped into the booth and then took aim at the target about twenty-five meters away from her. Her first shot hit the heart region on the picture of the man on the target. The next three shots all hit him square between the eyes. Diane had spent many years perfecting the art of shooting. She was proud that it was something she was good at. It made her feel just a little bit less vulnerable. Now, if her rapist came back to finish her off, she would be ready for him.

She practiced for a couple of hours until she was totally happy that she was hitting the target in the right places. Eventually satisfied that she was an accurate and precise shooter, she left the shooting range. But as she walked outside and opened the door of her car, she noticed a black sedan with darkened windows parked behind her. Finding it a little strange, she quickly unlocked her car and then started her engine. She drove away as quickly as she could, but the sedan kept following her. She sped up and tried to take a few back roads to shake him off. But the driver was very persistent. Eventually, after a fifteen-minute speed chase she turned down an alleyway in a village and managed to finally lose him. She wondered who he was and why he was following her. She was convinced that the man who raped her just did it to torment her and play with her. There was no doubt in her mind that he was a cold-blooded killer and would be back to complete the job.

Her knuckles were gripping the steering wheel of her car so tightly that they were white from the effort. She pulled up outside her house and walked up her garden path. She looked around her just to make sure that she was indeed alone. She unlocked her front door and was grateful to step into the familiar and warm interior of her home. Her cat, Sebastian rubbed himself against her legs and meowed for his food.

'Let us get you some tuna…'

Diane walked into her kitchen and looked for a tin of tuna in the pantry. She took one out, opened it and deposited the contents in the cat's food bowl.

Diane was dog tired and she desperately needed to unwind in a hot bath.

She poured herself a glass of wine and then walked upstairs and into the bathroom. She threw in a good portion of bubble bath and put on some soothing classical music. Lighting a few scented candles helped to calm her. She also added Lavender oil to her bath water. Ever since the rape, she had struggled to feel clean even after a bath.

She stepped in the bath and sighed with relief as she lay back and relished the sound of the bubbles popping around her. But she was feeling very vulnerable even though all her doors were locked, and her gun was on the table next to the bath. She could not completely relax if that man were out there. What did he want and why did he seem to know her? Although she could not get a good look at his face because of the balaclava he wore, surely, she would recognise his voice if she knew him?

Then her thoughts turned to Tiffany. She was so glad she had managed to convince her to avoid ECT. Although many people had reported positive results to the treatment, Diane was concerned about messing about with the brain and having memories wiped out. What if it deleted some of Tiffany's good memories making it even harder for her to heal from the depression? No, it was not the route to go. She felt it in her mind and her spirit. Diane knew that God was the only answer. He could completely heal Tiffany from her depression. The reason Diane knew this was because she had battled depression and anxiety for twenty years and only recently God had healed her completely and set her free.

Diane had always wanted to talk to Jason and find out what his intentions were towards Tiffany. He had been very erratic in his visits to the clinic and it greatly disturbed Diane.

Tomorrow she would phone him and find out what was going on. He needed to man up and be more of an emotional support for Tiffany. It was not right that he was being so aloof. She needed him now more than ever and this suicide attempt was really testing their love for one another. It would either make or break their relationship.

Diane sat up in the bath as she heard a crash downstairs. Her heart hammered so hard against her chest she was sure it would explode. She quietly stood up and reached for her dressing gown. She stepped out the bath and put on the gown. Diane picked up her gun and began to pad softly down the passage and continued to the stairs. Adrenalin rushed through her as she looked around her. Slowly, she walked down the stairs and into the living room area. She saw her crystal vase had been knocked off the table and had shattered on the floor. Her cat rubbed his soft furry body against her bare ankles. She put down her gun and sighed.

'Was that you, naughty boy?' The cat continued to purr. 'I was really attached to the particular vase.'

***

Ever since Diane had prayed for Tiffany, she was feeling much better. The heaviness that seemed to sit on her like a thick fog was now gone and for the first time in many years she began to feel hope. Was it possible that she could truly forgive herself and find her way out of the darkness? Diane had left a Bible with her and she was eager to read it. She opened it up on a random page and these scriptures seemed to jump out at her. *My lover spoke and said to me, arise my darling, my beautiful one, and come with me. See the winter is past*; the *rains are over and gone. Flowers appear on the earth; the season of singing has come; the cooing of doves is heard in our land.*

As the words sunk deep into her spirit, Tiffany felt a peace she had never dreamed possible. Could it be that God had really forgiven her for aborting her child? Yes, it must be true as she felt no condemnation from him. All she could feel was his unconditional love and acceptance of her.

She was deep in her own thoughts when Jason walked into the common room. It was a lovely surprise as she was not expecting to see him.

'Hi Tiff,' he said pulling her into a hug.

'How are you feeling?'

'Much better, thanks Jason. Diane came to visit.'

'That's good. I'm so glad as you need your women friends.'

Tiffany's eyes trembled with tears. 'But where have you been Jason?' You've hardly visited these past two weeks.'

'Let us sit down and have a chat about that as I need to explain myself to you.'

'Yes, we do need to talk,' answered Tiffany.

'Tiff, you know that I love you. But when you tried to take your life, I was so angry and resentful towards you. I did not understand how you could want to leave me behind to cope with all that pain and guilt. So, for a while I needed to stay away and get my head and emotions straight. I am sorry if I hurt you by not visiting enough, but I just could not cope with seeing you. Not at first anyway. But I have been seeing a counsellor and he has helped me work through my feelings. I am also feeling a huge amount of guilt over the abortion so there has been lots going on. But I have forgiven you and I don't resent you anymore.'

'Well, I never thought of it that way, Jason. Now that you have explained yourself, I can understand. I am sorry, I did not mean to hurt you through what I did. I was just in so much pain and I wanted it to end. I know it was stupid and selfish.'

'Well, it is all in the past now so let us forget about it and move forward with our lives. And, whilst we are on the topic of moving on, I want to ask you an important question.

Jason got down on one knee in front of Tiffany. Immediately her eyes filled with tears. 'Oh Jason…'

'Tiffany Joy Rogers, please will you do me the honour of becoming my wife?'

She threw herself into Jason's arms and squealed with delight.

'Yes, of course I will be your wife. I love you so much and what an incredible surprise.'

'I wanted to wait until you are out of hospital and take you to a romantic restaurant, but you just looked so sad today that I wanted to cheer you up. But as soon as you leave this clinic, I will take you out and celebrate our engagement with you. Don't worry, I also have a beautiful diamond ring to propose to you properly.'

'Oh, how exciting, that would be so lovely, Jason. I can't wait.'

The matron announced that visiting hours were over so the crowd in the common room began to disperse.

Tiffany walked up the stairs to her bedroom at the clinic with a spring in her step. Today had been a good day. She had experienced God's peace and now Jason had proposed to her. She could not wait to tell the girls her good news. With all the horrific events over the past few weeks it was great to have something positive and exciting to talk about.

***

Diane checked her reflection in the bathroom mirror, applied a coat of lipstick and brushed her long, blonde hair. She had booked an appointment with her doctor and was due to see him in an hour. The morning sickness had subsided, and Diane could not help but be amazed by the fact that she was pregnant. It was just so ironic. For so many years she had tried to conceive with Jeremy and now that he had gone, she had fallen pregnant by her rapist. Could it be a blessing? Was God granting her the child she had spent so many years praying for?

She walked out the door and relished the feeling of spring sunshine on her pale skin. As Diane walked to Wimbledon tube station, she contemplated the words Susan had spoken to her during the last Apples of Gold meeting. Could she forgive the man who had sexually abused her when she was just six years old? She knew that it was not possible in her own strength but with God's help perhaps she could do it. And, she would need to forgive her rapist too. As the assault was still fresh in her mind, the thought of forgiving him was too overwhelming.

She jumped onto the train and was relieved to find a seat by the door. Diane sat down, reached into her handbag, and took out her

Bible. It was time for her to get serious with God and she desperately wanted to connect with him. If she kept the child, she knew she would need God's wisdom and guidance. She opened her Bible and began to read:

'*For you created my inmost being, you knit me together in my mother's womb. I praise you because I am fearfully and wonderfully made; your works are wonderful, I know that full well.*'

God had confirmed to Diane that her child was ordained by him. It was not a mistake, it was a miracle and she would embrace and welcome this child. She closed her eyes and placed her hands protectively over her belly. Relief flooded over her. It was true what the Bible said, God did cause all things to work together for good.

Arriving at Earl's Court tube station, she jumped off the train and walked up the platform towards the High Street. Suddenly, her world seemed brighter. God had given her the assurance she needed, and she was looking forward to her appointment with the doctor.

Diane only had to wait a few minutes before she was ushered into the doctor's office. Hearing her child's heartbeat made her heart soar. The fetus was only seven weeks old and just a small pea sized dot on the monitor. She stared at the image on the screen and immediately a deep sense of peace settled into the recesses of her tortured soul. Could it be that this child would bring her the healing she so desperately craved? She felt as if God was reaching into her very soul and giving her a chance at happiness after all the tragedy she had suffered throughout her life. She closed her eyes as a single tear traced a path down her cheek. *Thank you, Lord* she whispered.

On her journey home, Diane's mind wandered to her friends. She could not wait to tell the other women her news. She was not sure how they would take it but all she knew was that the promise of a new life had burst into her world and turned it upside down. Now she had a future to look forward to and Diane was determined to turn her back on her sordid past and find the restoration that she craved. She wanted to be free of the chains that had held her bondage all through her life. It was time to face her demons head on by forgiving those who had tarnished her. For the first time since Susan had told her what she needed to do, Diane felt confident that she could forgive her perpetrators. It had taken her whole life to get her to this point and she knew it was a pivotal time where she could either become bitter and angry or she could find healing.

Diane ached to feel Jeremy's arms around her and at a moment like this she wished she could talk to him and tell her about everything she was experiencing. Jeremy would be relieved that she had found her way back to God as he was a committed Christian. Dare she hope that this new life would help to fill the void Jeremy had left behind?

***

Ever since Patrick had been in hospital, Charlotte found she could finally breath. For so many long and lonely years she had lived under his rule of physical and emotional abuse. The emotional roller coaster had taken its toll on her and she was desperate to escape his clutches.

He had been in the hospital for two weeks now and she still could not bring herself to go and visit him. The last time she had phoned the hospital, the doctor had said he had been moved out of ICU and the surgery had been a success. But he could not say if, or when he would wake up from the coma.

Charlotte was looking forward to the next Apples of Gold meeting which would be taking place that evening. She wanted to share with the group that she had come to a place in her life where although she was choosing to forgive Patrick, she was feeling brave enough to leave him. If he were to survive, she would do whatever it took to find her freedom and keep herself and her daughter safe.

When Charlotte arrived at the meeting at Pitshanger Community Centre, all her friends were already there. She hugged them all individually and then sat down next to Diane.

Susan walked into the room and closed the door behind her.

'Welcome ladies, its lovely to have you all here this evening. Who would like to be the first to share?

Diane raised her hand.

'I would,' she said.

'As you will all remember from our last meeting, I shared how I was attacked and raped at gunpoint. It was very frightening, and I am still trying to get over it. As my friends know, I have struggled to conceive a child for many years. Jeremy and I tried for over ten years and I thought the problem lay with me. But I was wrong as I have only just found out a couple of days ago that I am pregnant! As first I was shocked and unsure if I could go through with having the baby. But the more I thought about it, the more I realised that this could be a blessing. I prayed about it and God gave me a scripture to confirm that this life has been ordained by him. I have wrestled with my emotions but now I am finally at peace with it and I have decided to keep the baby.

'Wow, what an amazing testimony, Diane.' Said Susan. 'It is just so wonderful when God speaks so powerfully to us and gives us the assurance that we need.'

All the women in the room nodded. Charlotte reached for Diane's hand and squeezed it.

'Who else has some news to share?' Asked Susan.

Jessica raised her hand. 'I would like to say something,' she said.

'As you all know, my husband Craig and I have been going for counselling after the death of our daughter, Amy. At first Craig was reluctant to talk and I was worried that the counselling would have no effect on him. But a couple of days ago we went to our second session and he broke down in tears and poured his heart out. He is tormented by the guilt he feels. That is why he asked for a divorce. But seeing him like that…in so much pain, I realised that I could forgive him, and I do not want him to carry all that guilt. I told him we would work through our grief together and I'm hoping this breakthrough will save our marriage.'

'That's wonderful news,' Jessica. 'I will keep praying for your marriage.'

'Charlotte, what is the news regarding your husband?' Susan asked.

'The surgery was a success and he has now been moved out of ICU. But he is still in a coma and the doctor is not sure if he'll ever wake up.'

'How do you feel about that, Charlotte?'

'Ambivalent. I do not want to wish death on him but these past couple of weeks without him have showed me how much stress I have been living under. I cannot ever go back to that. I have decided that if he does pull through, I am going to leave him. The incredible part is that I no longer feel afraid. I think I have the courage now to do whatever it takes to get free. And, it is all thanks to this group and the friends I have made here. I think each one of you has inspired me.

'That is good to hear, Charlotte. God is so faithful, and he knew that you would need strong friends to help you break free.

Tiffany, it is so lovely to see you again. I believe you were released from the clinic yesterday. How are you feeling?'

'I am a new person, Susan. Diane came to visit me a few days ago and I decided to give my life to Jesus. She said the sinner's prayer with me and ever since that day, I feel completely different. All the suicidal thoughts have gone, and I feel hopeful about my future. I have so much peace in my heart now. I also have some really good news.'

Tiffany held out her left hand. A beautiful solitaire diamond ring sparkled on her finger.

'Look, I am now engaged. Jason proposed.'

'Oh, how wonderful,' said Susan. 'I have been praying that Jason would commit to you and I am so delighted that we have so much good news to share today.'

'Abigail, you seem awfully quiet. How are you doing?'

'Richard finally admitted to the affair and he has ended it. He says he's really sorry and wants to work on our marriage.' Abigail locked eyes with Jessica and then looked away quickly. I do still love him, and I want our marriage to work. I have been praying so much about it and I feel that with God's help I can forgive Richard and try to move on. My parents got divorced when I was a young child, and I do not want to put my own children through that trauma. I have also invested so much time and love into my marriage and we were very happy before Richard was unfaithful. I am hoping we can get back to how it was.'

'With God all things are possible, Abigail. I think you are very brave, and I admire your resolve and dedication to your marriage. I have seen marriages come back from the brink of death when both parties are committed to allowing God to do the work. It will take time, but you can both emerge out of this with a stronger marriage.

I think you can all graduate from this support group with flying colours. I am so proud of how far you have come. It is wonderful to see how you have supported and encouraged each other. You have all grown so much and although the Apples of Gold support group is always here if you need it, I think you are all well on your way to total healing. Let us close in prayer.

'Father God, thank you for these brave women. They were all hurting and struggling with various heartaches, but they chose to come here and seek your face. They have been vulnerable with strangers and that takes courage. I rejoice with them as they have embraced your healing and each other. Please bless them and give them wisdom in their future decisions, in Jesus name. Amen.

###

Printed in Great Britain
by Amazon